$\mathcal{B}\,\mathcal{A}\,C\,\mathcal{K}\,\mathcal{L}\,\mathcal{A}\,\mathcal{S}\,\mathcal{H}$

By David Penn

Bonker Books

www.BonkerBooks.com

A catalogue record from this book is available from the British Library

Printed in the United Kingdom

ISBN 978-0-9564941-9-1

www.Bonkerbooks.com

For the preservation of World Wildlife.

The murder of his fiancée, the girl who was the greatest person in the world to Brad Carter left him numb with grief and later with a burning hatred towards those responsible for her death. He vowed to avenge Michelle and sought the advice and help of a known Mafia Boss without realizing the mayhem he starts. Once set on the trail of the culprits Brad becomes sickened by the viciousness of the action he has set in motion. He attempts to put a stop to his vengeful actions only to find that once started, there is no way back.

Before you seek revenge first dig two graves.

Backlash

Contents

David Penn

PART ONE
Chapter 1

The market in St. Tropez was a lovely place to be on a Tuesday. Stalls were bulging with fresh flowers which perfumed the air with a fragrance nothing artificial could match. The fruit and vegetables displayed were as fresh as though just picked and the cheeses competed with the flowers to obtain dominance over the scented air.

Michelle was shopping for a special meal, her lover and (as yet not firm) fiancé was arriving for a week. It was two months since she had seen him and she was missing him dreadfully. She hugged herself in anticipation, argued cheerfully with the vendors, who knew her well and loved her cheerful and bubbling personality. Tall and dark with endless legs she swayed amongst the stalls, her rounded buttocks straining through denim shorts and her breasts fighting to get out of her skimpy t-shirt. Wolf whistles followed her... she laughed and blew kisses to the men who lusted after her.

Michelle had graduated from 'Le Universite de Paris 'with a degree in art. She painted in water colour during the off season months, scenes of the harbour and the lopsided buildings with their gaudy brickwork. They sold well and swiftly in the summer months as did her caricatures of the tourists. In a matter of five or ten minutes she would produce a drawing which was an uncanny likeness but emphasizing the comical side of the unfortunate individual. Shopping complete she slid on to her motor scooter and shot off in a cloud of smoke up the hill to her apartment. It was small, just one bedroom, a cozy lounge and a wet room where she could shower and make as much mess as she liked. The kitchen was compact but as neat as a new pin. As she busied herself sorting the meal for later she mused about the day she first met Brad. She was swimming off the beach some distance out and enjoying ducking and diving and generally messing about. Brad Carter had spotted her and dived in, swimming in a strong breast stroke under the surface. He suddenly surfaced alongside her and grabbed her around the waist, scared her to death.

'You're alright now, safe, I've got you, don't panic."

Michelle struggled out of his arms gasping. "You bloody fool what the hell do you think you're doing?" She back paddled away from him.

Brad looked shocked, "Sorry, I thought you were drowning."

"Do I look like I'm drowning you moron?" She was furious, sweeping her long hair back she glared venomously.

"Not really, but you don't swim very well."

'What! I'll have you know I am an expert, not like you, an expert in sexual harassment.'

"Race you to the beach then," Brad grinned, his teeth gleaming and eyes twinkling.

"Get stuffed."

"Oh alright, be like that, I was only trying to help." He swam slowly away, a sad and woebegone look on his face, he looked back twice. Perhaps he had really been worried she was in difficulties she thought, and he was a bit of a hunk.

She swam up to him, "Right, you're on..."

She set off slipping though the water in a strong American crawl, taking Brad by surprise. He soon caught her but tempered his strokes to stay just behind her. At the last fifty yards he speeded up and hit the beach just before her. He grabbed his towel and put it over her shoulders as she walked out of the water. They sat on the sand and dried off.

"Where would you like to go?"

"When...?"

'Tonight for dinner...?" Michelle looked at him stupefied, and then she laughed.

'If you don't take the cake you cheeky sod, tell me did you really think I was drowning?"

'Course not, just wanted to give you a cuddle you're a very beautiful girl you know."

She threw a handful of sand at him. They did go to dinner, that night and for many more. During the day they swam and sunbathed, ate seafood and ice cream and gradually fell deeply in love. Michelle became entranced with Brad. He was kind, considerate, and funny. After a week she invited him for dinner.

"No strings," she said coyly.

"Only if you insist…"

They made love deep into the night and early morning, not able to get enough of each-other. The occasions when Brad had to leave were agony for them both, but, when able, he drove from Paris and stayed as long as he could. Life was sweet.

Four months had passed since that Christmas, that wonderful Christmas, a cozy mountain paradise high in the Aravis Range, skiing the Pistes and managing to include every bar on the way down. The sun setting the icicles shone as brightly as the sparkle in their eyes. The nights were long, Brad loving her gently, persuasively and yet insistent coaxing her to the edge of the precipice and toppling into the void together. Michelle shook her head and came back to reality she doused the salad in cold water. Then the Phone rang.

"Hi darling are you ok?"

"I'm fine, where are you? Don't tell me you can't come. I miss you so much."

"Of course I'm coming silly just be a bit late, about an hour or so, explain later. Love you to bits." He hung up.

4

Michelle looked sadly at the table and poured herself a glass of wine.

Chapter 2

Brad eased the BMW out of the congested traffic in Digne and accelerated towards Grasse, some 120km distant. He had purposefully chosen this route in order to stop off in Grasse, to buy Michelle her favourite perfume and to enjoy the invigorating change from the pulsating traffic of Paris, along the winding mountain route across the Alps.

Brad Carter was thirty, tall, fit and a successful journalist. Born of English parents in British Columbia he had started as a 'carbon hound' in the offices of the Vancouver Telegraph. A love of journalism and a 'talent' of being in the wrong place at the right time had swept him into a senior position with the Quebec Etoile Matin where he soon became proficient in French. Anxious for a change he secured a post with Paris Match, the leading French Magazine, contributing regular articles of the weird and wonderful who thronged St. Tropez in the peak season interviewing and photographing and encouraging them to show off their talents, and lack of. He spun the wheel and overtook a rumbling juggernaut, elbowing back into the right lane as the corner approached. He lit a cigarette and slid a cd into the player. There was little traffic on the road. The kilometers sped by so much better than the miles that took so long to diminish. Kilometers disappeared fast, sixty more to Grasse. He frowned at the image in the rear mirror. A small Renault turbo lay behind him, bright red and close. Too close. 'Be in my bloody boot next' he growled. The car was only two or three feet behind him, the engine blipping as the driver swung out and back in again in an effort to overtake. Brad refused to speed up on this road, it would be suicide. If he slowed the Renault would smash into his rear end. The road twisted and writhed along the mountain edge a drop of 500 feet to the offside, solid rock on the other. Brad flicked on his hazard lights and glowered in the mirror. The Renault was glued to his bumper.

'Damn all French drivers to hell' he thought, tight lipped. The next curve was slightly broader and left a little more visibility, the Renault swung out and shrieked by only inches from the edge of the road, cutting back suddenly into the correct side. Brad braked to avoid being clipped. The car whipped around the bend and out of sight. Brad breathed again and lit a cigarette. The smashed bicycle lay across the road a kilometer ahead. Front wheel spinning above the mutilated frame. A young boy lay crumpled against the rock strewn bank. Shocked, Brad pulled up with a squeal of brakes and climbed out of the car. There was no-one else about, no sign of the Renault. The road deserted.

"Christ the bastards killed him and didn't stop."

The boy was about fourteen, dressed in shorts and a t-shirt. The cycle, an expensive model looked new. He lay crumpled and unconscious, left leg twisted unnaturally under his body, an arm flopped across his face. Certain the boy was dead Brad carefully moved his arm and looked into a pallid and bruised face. He was still breathing, pulse fast and shallow. He was bleeding profusely from a deep cut on his inner thigh. Grabbing his first aid kit from the car he applied a tourniquet above the wound, wrapping a pebble in a bandage, placing it beneath as near to the pressure point as he could remember, the bleeding eased. He bandaged the wound. Cursing the desolation of the area, phoning for help would take too long. Brad tenderly straightened the leg and lifted the boy across the back seat. He was slim, heavy and awkward. The leg was definitely broken and the kid was in deep shock. Stopping only to shove the cycle into the boot, Brad set off as quickly as he dared. Grasse was the nearest town. Occasionally glancing at the inert form he was relieved to hear an occasional groan of pain. Where was the hospital, he didn't know Grasse. As he drove into Grasse he was relieved to see a blue H sign with arrows towards the hospital. The entrance lay back from the main road, ignoring the no entry signs he drove straight up to it. An angry Porter approached waving his arms.

Brad opened the rear door. "Accident, the boy has a broken leg! Stop waving your arms about and get a stretcher."

Within minutes the lad was transferred to a trolley, a nurse alongside and he was wheeled into the emergency room. Brad relaxed. The Porter returned and directed Brad to the parking area and asked him to return to the reception.

At reception Brad outlined the situation but said nothing about the Renault, he didn't want to become more involved than he was already. He pushed aside twinges of conscience. He left his name and Michelle's address. The doctor confirmed a broken leg, bruising and abrasions but no sign of any internal complications. He had been given a blood transfusion, had recovered consciousness and said he had been knocked over by a fast moving red car which did not stop.

The Doctor smiled, "at least that dispels any possibility of you being the guilty person."

Brad was shocked, that hadn't occurred to him. "What is the boys' name?"

"Vittorino," he consulted his notes, "Paul Vittorino, we are trying to contact his parents. You can safely leave all the details to us, thank you on behalf of his parents we must inform the Gendarmarie such an act is very serious in France."

Brad left, feeling guilty at saying nothing about the Renault. He rang Michelle to say he would be late, and felt even keener to gather her in his arms. As he wound his way out of the hilly roads of Grasse a large Total garage displayed a reduction on each litre of petrol. He needed petrol but admitted that it was the sight of a red Renault Turbo with the front end jacked up that decided him to drive in. The car was being hammered by a greasy mechanic sprawled beneath it. The front wing was buckled and bent across the wheel, the tyre superficially shredded. A young swarthy man, slim and flashily dressed, stood impatiently glancing at his watch and occasionally looking over his shoulder towards the town. It had to be the same car. Brad climbed out and filled his tank, still watching. The mechanic had cleared the bent wing and started to change the wheel. Brad caught some of the conversation.

"The spare will do. I will get another tyre later, and would the mechanic please get a move on."

Under the pretense of writing a cheque Brad copied down a rough description of the man and carefully noted the registration number. The suffix was 06. So he came from Nice. Brad drove straight to the Gendarmarie.

Chapter 3

A burly sergeant listened to the facts that Brad outlined and was able to confirm matters with the hospital. He was asked to wait in an adjoining room. Half an hour later an important looking little man came bustling in and seating himself behind a desk, he proceeded to type out a statement making sure of every detail. Brad was asked to read and sign each copy and retain one himself.

"Merci Monsieur," the Gendarme beamed and offered his hand. "You have performed a valuable public service we shall be in touch when we have arrested the villain. Inspector Dubois will be taking the case, he is with the Surete, had it been a traffic accident we would have handled the matter, but as the driver didn't stop, it's a crime, a serious crime, au revoir."

Brad left, over 3 hours late and swung on to the Grasses-Cannes autoroute. Suddenly he remembered the perfume, he had completely forgotten it. He swore, it was too late now, he'd never get back to town in under an hour. Stabbing the button on the Peage he snarled into the fast last and put his foot down. The engine responded gratefully, resentful of the miles of gear changing and slower speeds. He sped along the smooth surface, the setting sun hot and orange soothed his annoyance. An hour later he coasted into St. Maxime and followed the spit of land to St. Tropez.

Michelle was worried. The afternoon had passed quickly cleaning and tidying the small apartment. She stood bathed in the late April sun streaming through the window. She wiped a drop of perspiration off the end of her nose. 'Didn't these builders realize how hot it got, especially through glass, fancy putting a window facing west in the business part of the house. Flicking back her long hair she looked around and checked all was well.

Coquilles Jacques, chilling in the fridge. Two bottles of Macon wine, steaks marinating in red wine and garlic. Salad swimming happily in a bowl of chilled water and ice cubes. She stripped and dived under the shower and relaxed. The streaming jets calming her excitement. It was nearly eight thirty. Brad had promised late afternoon, it was hardly that, he was late. She checked her watch again and peered out of the window. She had dressed carefully, choosing a yellow sun-dress that set her dark hair and sun-tanned limbs off to perfection. A single necklet of fine gold supported a ruby pendant, Brads Christmas present nestling and flickering fire in the cleavage of her full breasts. As his car drew up all her good intentions of greeting him serene and seductive, were thrown to the wind. She wrenched open the door and ran to him before he could close the car door behind him. He laughed and swept her up in his arms.

"I've been so worried," she said between kissing him, "You're late, where have you been?" She kissed him again and snuggled close as they walked into the apartment. They sat, curled up on the settee and Brad told her everything that had happened over the last four months and also about the accident and why he had been so late.

Michelle kissed him. "My hero you saved the boy's life, we must ring tomorrow to see how he is." They ate perfunctorily, their interest only in each other. Michelle forgot the ice cream melbas which slowly dissolved in the fridge. It was 3am before they climbed into bed and spent the rest of the night locked together floating in a world of love and fierce possession.

Michelle woke late in the morning, sleepy eyed, her hair tumbling across her face she carefully eased herself away from the sleeping Brad, sliding a long leg out of bed. She was almost out when a strong arm encircled her waist and dragged her back. Squealing and giggling, it was another hour before she tried again.

"What do you want for breakfast?" She demanded kissing Brad on the nose.

"You," the muffled reply came as he nuzzled her neck.

Finally Michelle escaped into the shower and it was left to Brad to answer the insistent ring on the door bell. Tousled and shrugging on a robe he opened the door, to be faced with a small immaculately dressed man in his late forties. His thinning hair brushed close to his head and a carefully groomed moustache setting off a florid and serious face. His eyes were bright and bird like, he swiftly assessed Brad from top to toe.

"Pardon monsieur," he gestured apologetically at Brads' appearance. "I will return later, but he made no move to leave.

"No problem. What can I do for you?"

"My name is Dubois, Inspector Dubois, of the Surete." He offered his card which appeared like magic in his tubby hand.

Christ, he looks like Hercule Poirot, Brad thought. "You had better come in Inspector."

Dubois walked into the room nodding his appreciation.

Michelle bounced out of the bathroom hardly covered in a fluffy bath towel, a bright yellow shower cap perched ridiculously on her head, black hair falling out over her eyes. Seeing Dubois she grabbed frantically at the towel. "Merde," she shrieked and shot into the bedroom.

The Inspectors eyes twinkled. "Formidable," he breathed appreciatively.

Brad glared and drew up a chair. "How can I help you?" he asked firmly.

"The boy Vittorino, victim of the hit and run accident you were involved in."

"I was not involved in the accident," retorted Brad indignantly, "the accident had already happened when I got there."

"Yes, yes of course, a slip of the tongue."

"You don't look like a person who makes a slip of the tongue." Brad noticed the Inspectors eyes flitting around the room, noting what he saw. What the hell was he suspicious about?

"How is the boy?" Brad was intent on concentrating the police officers attention.

."Broken leg, abrasions, bruises," Dubois shrugged, "he is very lucky, there should be no complications. He could have been killed."

"It seems unusual to say the least, for an inspector from the Surete to be involved in such an incident?" Brad was curious, not convinced of the true reason for Dubois visit. Serious as it was, the accident didn't call for the big guns.

"I am attached to the Var region for another reason. There is a possibility that there is a connection. How well do you know the boys' father?"

The question startled Brad. "I have never met his father, wouldn't know him if he fell in my lap. What on earth makes you think I do? I gave all the information to the Gendarme, at the Station. You must have seen my statement, before I found the boy in the road I had never set eyes on him. What are you getting at Inspector?" Brad went on quietly. "Where's the big problem? "You would be far better employed tracking down the driver of the Renault, he's the bastard you

15

should be questioning, not me."

"Oui, certainment," agreed Dubois, "that is all being taken care of, we may ask you to identify the man later."

"I can identify the man I saw at the garage, but that doesn't mean to say he was the driver who hit the boy. I didn't see him do that."

Dubois nodded.

Michelle emerged from the bedroom looking radiant. She pulled a face at Brad. "You could have told me we had visitors," she pouted.

"Bon Jour Monsieur," Dubois rose to his feet and took her slim hand as though it was a fragile flower. "Enchante Mamselle." He smiled and meant it.

"Café...?"

"Non Merci I must be going, you will be here for some time yet?"

"Unfortunately only another week or so, but you may have my office address in Paris and my home telephone number." Brad handed Dubois his card.

"Merci monsieur, mamselle." Dubois shook hands and left.

"What the hell do you make of that?" Brad frowned. "The Surete poking around asking damn fool questions, something fishy here."

Michelle sniffed, "I don't smell fish."

"Just an expression," he grinned, "You look edible."

"You look a mess," she replied, "off you go while I make coffee."

Chapter 4

Their day was spent wandering around St. Tropez which Michelle knew so well. She introduced Brad to many friends alongside the quay, many busy painting and sketching, gawped at by tourists from all around the world. The harbour was relatively free of large shipping, it would be a little later when the very wealthy tied up their multi million pound yachts and commandeered the quay side. They swam all afternoon and lazed on the gravelly sand of Tahiti beach, and filled themselves with seafood at the Marina restaurant in the early evening.

Happy in their world the days passed quickly. It was four days later that Michelle peered out of the window. "We have more visitors," she called to Brad.

"Not that bloody police Inspector again?"

"Don't think so, too posh for Police."

Brad joined her at the window. Parked outside was a large Mercedes 500 SEI, shining like wet coal. A burly man, his muscular build straining from his chauffeurs uniform looked around as he closed the car door and adjusted his cap.

"Christ, he looks a toughie," breathed Brad.

The chauffeur walked up the short pathway and rang the bell. Brad opened the door. He looked at the man with a puzzled frown. The huge man took up most of the doorway. Dark curly hair protruded from beneath the cap and his face was typically Mediterranean, dark and swarthy with heavy eyebrows and a hooked nose. His mouth was thin lipped and hard so it was a surprise when his face lit up into a very happy smile giving an immediate air of pleasure.

"M'sieur Carter...?" He asked removing his cap.

Brad nodded, still awed by the sheer size of the man. Brad was 6ft 3 inches but he felt insignificant against this character.

"Don Vittorino sends you his warmest wishes." Seeing the puzzled look on Brads' face he went on, "his son was the boy who you saved after he was knocked down. Don Vittorino is very grateful and tells me I must make sure that you join him for the weekend," he glanced at Michelle who was peering over Brads shoulder, "of course that includes your lovely lady." He grinned.

"That is very kind but we are quite busy. My holiday you see."

the big man's face fell. "Don Vittorino will be very unhappy if you cannot come. I was told not to take no for an answer," his face saddened, "I am to collect you in the car," He gestured over his shoulder, "perhaps at six o'clock, whatever is best for you?" He smiled the infectious smile again.

Brad jumped as Michelle kneed him in the backside,

which he took to be the female way to tell him to agree.

"Very well," Brad smiled, "we shall be delighted, did you say the weekend?"

"Yes I was told to say you must stay." The giant grinned happily again. Placing his cap back on his head he saluted cheerfully and hurried back to the car in case there was a change of mind.

"Well, what do you know?" Brad gripped Michelle firmly by the ear, "Just what does a knee in the bum mean?"

"Could mean anything," Michelle wriggled away, "you knew though," she chuckled, "I'd love to go, with a car like that what must his house be like?"

"It's only because you fancy the chauffeur."

"Ooooooh…" she breathed with relish.

True to his word the car drew up right on 6 pm. Good job it hadn't been any earlier thought Brad, the time that Michelle had taken to decide what to wear and preparing herself. Finally she had decided on a sheer white dress that clung to her figure, plunging low at the back and fastened high at the throat, taut across her full breasts it did more to emphasize them than a plunging neckline. She had offset it all with her favourite ruby necklet. A small figure peered from the rear seat of the car and Brad recognized Paul. He was astonished.

"Out of hospital so soon…?"

Paul had his right arm in a sling and his leg was

plastered from ankle to thigh. There were grazes on his face which were no longer angry. "I am being looked after at home," he said happily," my father has hired a nurse to look after me, but I am not too bad."

He shrugged and wrinkled his nose at the leg stretched out in front of him. He and Michelle took to each other immediately and chattered away in explosive French, laughing and giggling.

The car sped silently through Port Grimaud and St Maxime eating up the kilometres to the autoroute. They arrived at the northern part of Cannes in forty minutes. "It takes me over an hour." Brad thought enviously. They skirted Cannes and climbed in to the low Alpes, the azure sky a backdrop to the sea which shimmered and sparkled. Finally, they turned in front of two immense wrought iron gates set in a picturesque but functional solid wall, eight feet high. From nowhere a man appeared inside the gate, dressed in dark slacks and a polo necked jumper. He nodded at the chauffeur and the gates opened silently. They purred along a well-kept drive and Brad spotted two other men standing idly in the trees and bushes. They seemed alert and inquisitive.

"You seem to be well protected here Paul?"

Paul shrugged, "My father is an important man. We have many valuable items in the house and it is necessary that we have protection."

"What does your father do?" Michelle asked.

"He has many businesses, spends a long time away from home sometimes."

"Does your mother go with him?" Michelle thought he looked sad.

"I did not know my real mother," Paul said quietly, "she died many years ago. My father has Sophia, but they are not married."

"Oh! I see," Michelle decided not to probe any more, Paul looked quietly unhappy. As they neared the house Brad glanced at Michelle.

"Some pad," he murmured.

The car stopped in front of a huge wide entrance flanked by two marble pillars. The chauffeur nimbly opened the door and with Gallic charm assisted Michelle. He then reached inside and lifted Paul as though he was weightless and carefully sat him in the waiting wheelchair.

"No crutches yet," Paul complained.

"Two more weeks," the chauffer said firmly.

He was wheeled away by a young nurse dressed in immaculate white. "See you soon," Paul called as he disappeared in the house.

As the chauffeur carried their cases, Don Vittorino, appeared.

Tall and slim he was dressed elegantly in a navy blue blazer and a snow white open necked shirt, a cravat

22

knotted casually around his neck. Paul reckoned he was in his early fifties. His hair was dark and graying at the temples, clean shaven apart from a thin moustache which graced his upper lip. He smiled warmly showing even white teeth and took Michelle's hand, raising it to his lips and brushing her finger-tips.

"Enchante Mamselle, welcome to my home." He turned to Brad and shook his hand, his grip firm and sincere." It is a great pleasure to meet such a man." Brad felt embarrassed at the emotion in Don Vittorino's voice. "You must be weary after your journey, please," he beckoned to a petite maid, "my home is yours, when you have freshened up please join me for an aperitif."

He left them to the girl who led them through a magnificent hallway and climbed a curved staircase. They both gazed around in awe. The walls were hung with portraits, original and valuable his practiced eye told him. The whole building though massive and magnificent still retained a warm and welcome atmosphere. The bedroom afforded a magnificent view across the bay, the sea sparkling as though scattered with diamonds, the islands of Lerins clearly visible. Two doors were open on to a marble tiled balcony with dusky pink wrought iron railings. The room was decorated in pink and blue, with two large single beds placed at a discreet distance from each other, a huge bathroom with a sunken bath and a shower room. A vase of freshly picked blooms graced the table. Michelle was enchanted she examined everything, thrilled as a child on Christmas morning.

23

"I could stay here for the rest of my life," she said bouncing on the bed.

Brad looked thoughtful. "It certainly is incredible," he said. "You don't get to earn this from honest toil. I bet there is another side to Vittorino, even if he won the lottery that wouldn't buy the bloody roof. Did you see the ceiling in the atrium?"

"Don't look a gift horse in the mouth." laughed Michelle poking her tongue out.

After half an hour they made their way down and were shown into the lounge, which was larger than the whole of Michelle's apartment. Don Vittorino, now dressed more formally, stood at a lavishly stocked bar which took up the whole of one corner. They were joined by the loveliest woman Michelle had ever set eyes on. Tall and slender, her pale and flawless complexion offset with jet black hair swept tightly back from her face. She had the hauteur of the aristocrat and the suppressed fire typical of the Spanish. High cheekbones and deep green eyes smiled as she extended her hand to Michelle, and then to Brad. Don Vittorino introduced them.

"This is Sophia, the lady of my home," he said tactfully as he poured drinks, and throughout dinner he was the epitome of charm and intrigued his guests with the history of some of his possessions. The meal was perfect and the effect of Lafitte Rothschild 1916 wine left Brad and Michelle feeling very contented. Sophia and Michelle left the men to their cigars and strolled around the gardens in the late evening warmth. Michelle noticed two men hovering at discreet distances, but Sophia appeared not to notice them.

Don Vittorino puffed life into his cigar, "I have not had an opportunity of telling you how much I am in your debt," He looked sincerely at Brad.

Embarrassed Brad dismissed the words. "I was only too happy to have come along. Anyone decent would have done the same."

"That is not so," Don Vittorino insisted, "your care and attention meant that my son suffered less than he would have done. The person who so callously left him for dead will be brought to book. Paul is my only son, his mother is dead. He is the heir to all this," he waved his cigar to envelope the room, "and more besides. His good health and safety are most important, that is why we are well protected as you may have noticed."

Brad grinned, "I should have thought your chauffeur alone was enough."

Don Vittorino laughed. "He is, shall we say, a pillar of strength and a very valuable asset. Very gentle most of the time, but deeply possessive of Paul and Sophia, myself as well, for which I have good reason to be thankful."

Brad said nothing, hoping his host would elaborate on the last remark, but he did not. Throughout the meal he had hoped to gather some inkling of how Vittorino became possessed of such vast wealth. The newsman in him smelled an interest, but he was too cautious to ask outright. His thoughts were interrupted by Don Vittorino speaking.

"I do not wish to embarrass you further by pursuing the matter but I would like to emphasize that I shall forever be in your debt. It is part of my culture you see, not just an idle thank you. If there is anything I can do for you, funds, contacts, opportunities, help of any sort, I insist you contact me."

Brad shifted in his chair, uncomfortable, 'he does go on so, he thought, 'anyone would have done the same and perhaps bought him a pint.' He smiled.

Don Vittorino passed a small gilt edged business card across the table, there was nothing printed on it, except a telephone number. "That is my personal number. No-one else will answer. Now..." He rose to his feet before Brad could reply. "I have always fancied myself at snooker or pool as you north Americans call it. Do you play?"

Not bothering to explain the difference between a north American and Englishman he accepted with alacrity. He used to be good, but hadn't played for years.

"Come," said his host, you can teach me some wrinkles."

He walked out of the room into a huge games room, the lighting subdued except for the canopied lights above two billiard tables, set up and ready to play. Brad selected a cue from the rack and stripped off his coat. A maid discreetly entered carrying a tray of drinks. Brad wondered how she had been briefed.

Chapter 5

The next morning they slept late. Brad woke with a muzzy head but received no sympathy from Michelle who was her usual effervescent self. She badgered him to swim in the diamond shaped pool which scintillated in the brilliant sunshine beneath their balcony. Finally he gave in and donned a pair of shorts and plunged bleary eyed into the crystal clear water. Ten energetic lengths cleared his hangover and he ducked Michelle to pay her out for nagging. As he surfaced there was a round of applause from the poolside. Paul had arrived, leaning forward in his wheelchair slapping his good leg and laughing. His nurse hovered nearby.

"Do you swim?"

"Only when I have two legs," he gestured with disgust at his plaster," but I can't swim like that."

"When you are fit I'll help you." He smiled at the eagerness on Pauls' face.

Michelle was floating serenely on her back, her black hair swirling around her head, her white costume almost transparent in the sunlight.

Brad grabbed hold of her, "You're positively indecent," he gloated, pulling her under.

"I haven't noticed you complaining before." She

spluttered, pulling away her strong strokes powerful and graceful.

They emerged to a sumptuous breakfast, served on the terrace. Paul joined them, and although he had already eaten he helped them demolish the food.

"I thought you French only ate croissants and coffee for breakfast," grinned Brad awed by Pauls' capacity.

"A vicious rumour," he replied, his mouth full of toast.

Sophia joined them after they had showered and dressed, looking resplendent in a colourful full length silken sheath dress, she apologized for Don Vittorino.

"He had important business early today," she explained, "but should return for lunch. Perhaps you would like to see our home and the grounds?"

Michelle was delighted and Brad was also keen to have an opportunity to assess more information. Eight bedrooms with en suite bathrooms, the walls holding valuable pictures and watercolours they were amazing. The master bedroom was more like a self-contained flat with an adjoining study and sun room. The ground floor boasted a huge dining room, library and magnificent semi-circular lounge and doors leading on to the terrace overlooking the pool. There was a massive games room where Brad had managed to beat Don Vittorino at snooker and another room, the door securely locked it was not included in the tour. As always it is the unobtainable which is of the main interest and Michelle speculated later as to the ominous contents of the secret room as she called it.

"Probably full of dirty washing," Brad chuckled, "why are women so damned nosey?"

Paul took them around the huge grounds, his nurse dutifully pushing his wheelchair, perspiring in the morning heat. The whole estate was encircled by a huge wall with small brick built lodges nestling in the trees. Paul didn't mention them. The gardens, beautifully tended were a mass of colour with spring blossoms. An elderly gardener busy as they walked by, he didn't look up. At the rear of the house a man stood, leaning against the outhouses. A well-built pen, containing four kennels was nearby. The man held four Doberman Pinschers on strong leads. They made no sound but bared their teeth in a soundless snarl. A word from the man and they settled down with suspicious eyes. He acknowledged Paul with a nod.

"I wouldn't want to meet them on a dark night." Michelle was shaken by the thought and drew closer to Brad.

"They run free at night," said Paul. "each dog knows where to guard, so it is not safe to be out here after dark without one of the men."

Don Vittorino joined them for drinks at noon, resplendent in a white linen suit he was a perfect host, entertaining Michelle with a history of Genoa when Monaco was part of the Italian possessions. Michelle knew part of the history, and Brad not at all, but the detail explained by Vittorino showed him to be well read on the subject. As lunch was concluded he produced two beautifully wrapped packages and passed one too Michelle and the other to Brad. He looked for a long moment at Brad.

"A small token to express my gratitude, and for your charming company..." He looked at Sophia who smiled.

Embarrassed they thanked Vittorino but didn't open the gifts. He waved away their thanks and explained that the car would be ready for their return whenever they wished. He would say his goodbyes now, as Sunday or not, he had much to do.

"You are welcome any time, just ring and you will be picked up."

As they were driven homeward, the same burly chauffeur threading his way through the traffic, Michelle couldn't wait to open her package. She was astounded to find a beautiful solid gold Cartier wrist watch, the delicate face studded with tiny jewels, the band and integral part of the watch gleaming gold as well. "Mon Dieu" she gasped, "it must have cost a fortune."

Equally astonished Brad, unwrapped his gift. A solid gold Rolex Oyster nestled in the box, again with a solid gold band. He looked at Michelle, "God knows how much these cost." He breathed, amazed at such generosity. "Whatever does that man do to possess all that wealth?"

Michelle recovered swiftly, her delight rapidly overcoming any feeling of shock. She eagerly clipped it around her wrist, admiring the flickering lights of the jewels as they caught the rays of the sun.

Brad adjusted the Rolex, "be fine in the rain," he grinned, "waterproof to 150 metres."

When the car drew up outside the apartment Brad offered the chauffeur a drink which was politely refused. He touched his cap with a broad smile at Michelle and eased his frame back into the driving seat. The Mercedes slid silently away.

"What an experience," Brad threw himself into an easy chair and pulled Michelle on to his lap. She kissed him. "Wasn't that clever of you to rescue small boys what a wonderful place that is. I wonder what Don does for a living?"

"Nothing, it would seem, must take all his energy deciding how to spend his money."

Happily discussing their weekend their mood was destroyed by a ring on the bell. Inspector Dubois stood on the doorstep. Brad was angry and showed it.

"What the hell do you want?" He glowered at Dubois. "You are becoming a bloody nuisance, on a Sunday as well." He made no attempt to invite the Inspector inside.

"My apologies for disturbing you," Dubois smiled apologetically, "if I could take a few moments of your time it's important believe me." Hesitantly Brad stood aside.

Michelle was more charming and pulled a chair forward. "How can we help?"

The Inspector smoothed his moustache. "Previously you told me you had never met Don Vittorino. It would seem that is not the truth. I have reason to believe you spent some time at his home and have just returned." He looked severely at Brad.

Brad narrowed his eyes, he was very angry this pompous little man not only invaded their privacy with fatuous and irrelevant questions, but now had the effrontery to accuse him of being a liar.

"Look here Inspector I don't know what all this is about. I told you I had never met Don Vittorino and that was true, then. Since I last saw you we received an invitation to join him for the weekend, the reason being that he wished to thank me for assisting his son Paul after the accident. We have spent a very enjoyable weekend at his home. He was most charming and I can assure you that unless you can come up with a bloody good reason for badgering Michelle and I, and obviously following my movements without any justification, I shall boot your backside straight through that door, police or no bloody police."

Brad stood up clenching and unclenching his fists, struggling to contain his feelings. Michelle had never seen him so angry. She stepped in before Dubois was sent flying through the door.

"Brad, Brad, sit down and don't make a scene. I'm

sure the Inspector has a good reason for asking these questions, haven't you?" She turned anxiously towards Dubois. The Inspector nodded understandingly.

"Please," he appealed to Brad who sat down still fuming. "I have been put in charge of the VAR Region, because I am, as you say, a new broom and it is hoped that I can sweep clean. My responsibilities include narcotics and there is a huge problem along the coast of France. Everyone knows where the problem lays but there is no proof."

"What has this got to do with us?" Brad was still angry.

"Nothing, directly, I am sure," answered Dubois, "but is has a lot to do with Vittorino."

Michelle's eyes opened wide, "I can't believe that, he is so charming, his wife or rather his mistress," she corrected herself, "is beautiful and delightful, drugs are so," she searched for the right word, "filthy," there is no sign of that."

"I don't doubt that Mamaselle, such activities are never obvious, but there is no doubt it is true. Don Vittorino is the 'Capo...the head of the Mafia. He is a powerful and influential man with his tentacles into crime, prostitution, narcotics and gambling. In fact any activity that makes money, lots of money, you name it he is somehow behind it. We have been able to collect evidence over the years but always, before anything can be done a witness disappears or suddenly dies there is never enough evidence to proceed on. We occasionally arrest a drug runner and sometimes a prostitute, but they are small fry, we want the head of the snake."

Brad and Michelle sat shocked.

Dubois continued. "There is a twenty hour, surveillance on Don Vittorino and his home that is how I knew you had been to visit him. Everything he does, wherever he goes, is noted and watched."

"But does Sophia know anything about this." Brad asked.

Dubois smiled, "She is the Madame, runs the girls, as far as we know there are twenty or so call girls. Beautiful, really beautiful women, very highly paid. They are contacted by Sophia by coded messages and meet wealthy business men, politicians, eminent persons who would never want their activities disclosed. How they are paid, sometimes thousands of euros, we don't know, where they meet their client is also unknown, they are clever girls. As you know prostitution is not exactly tolerated in France, but many high class hotels turn a blind eye and are no doubt paid for their co-operation."

The sincerity of Dubois, coupled with the obvious wealth of Vittorino made sense to Brad.

"That answers a lot of questions. I said to Michelle that you don't get money like that by honest means."

"I could not be sure that you were in no way involved, you must excuse my persistence, but I need to investigate every possibility. Is there anything you can offer in the way of help, anything in his home which was unusual?" Dubois looked at Brad hopefully.

The thought of using Don Vittorinos generosity to lay him open to police action was obnoxious to Brad. He shook his head, "nothing but luxury, superb taste and obvious signs that intruders are not welcome."

"What signs?"

"Massive walls around the property guards patrolling the grounds, vicious dogs after dark. Understandable when you see the possessions in the place."

Dubois rose to his feet. "Please excuse my intrusion I shall not bother you again." He extracted a business card from his waistcoat pocket. You have my number in Paris. This number will reach me locally. If ever there is anything that would help, he smiled and took his leave.

Chapter   6

The days passed quickly, far too quickly, Brad was scheduled to cover the Cannes Film Festival from the 16th to 27th May. When he left Michelle felt empty. She tried to busy herself catching up with neglected housework, wandering aimlessly around the villa. Brad phoned to tell her where he was staying and promised long weekend trips just as soon as he could.

With that at least to console her, she threw herself into work. Collecting her portfolio of paintings, easel and sketching pads she secured them precariously on her Honda and set off for the quayside. She was surprised to see how many new boats were now gracing the harbour, just a short time and so many things had changed. The tourist season was under way. She set herself up and got busy finishing a large oil painting of the harbour, annoyed that a small fishing boat which had formed the focal point was now hidden by a huge sea going yacht gleaming with varnished timbers and brass fittings. The next few days passed quickly and profitably, her paintings sold well and crowds of tourists were eager to have their portraits drawn and signed with Michelle's flamboyant signature dated St. Tropez.

"So much better than a butter dish dear," said one woman to her husband who watched admiringly while

Michelle sketched.

During the next week two letters and numerous phone calls from Brad cheered her up. She arrived at her pitch on a Monday evening. She noticed that the brassy yacht had left and that another large one, flying the German flag had arrived. Mondays were never as busy as the rest of the week so Michelle joined Andre, a bearded French artist who dressed, it seemed, in the same jeans and faded multi-coloured jumper throughout the year. She could never remember him looking any different. A grubby bandana kept his uncombed long hair back from his craggy face and a huge medallion was suspended around his neck on a solid gold chain. He specialized in miniatures, tiny reproductions of everything he could see and many that his fertile imagination could conjure up. Seemingly disinterested in whether he sold them or not, he spent hours of deep concentration, a frown furrowing his brow. Occasionally he would break off and cadging a part of Michelle's sketch pad would cruelly caricature an innocent tourist unlucky enough to have an unusual face. The result pleased the tourist but created spiteful hilarity in his companions, always ready to see the worst in others.

Michelle told him he was wicked, but Andre would chuckle and wave a fifty euro note in her face. They regularly joined each other for an afternoon break, Michelle drinking coffee whilst Andre dispatched three or four beers, making the excuse that he was allergic to coffee. Michelle suggested that tea would be a good alternative but Andre would screw up his face, horror struck. They were very strong friends, Andre adored her and Michelle felt comfortable that he was near, aware of how protective he was. He called her fleur, insisting that she was the one bright bloom in the whole shabby garden. He would occasionally catch her eye, his raised eyebrows and rolling eyes leaving no doubt what he meant. She found it hard not to giggle.

The German yacht was always gone when Michelle arrived, but returned regularly around six o'clock, coming in stern first the lines and gangplank expertly secured. She had little opportunity to study the occupants, but then she wasn't interested so it was with surprise, that she glanced up and saw three men watching her. They looked typical of the fraternity who spent their time messing about on boats. In their thirties dressed in shorts and t-shirts, with the inevitable glass in their hands, they stood alongside the after guardrail watching her with interest. She became uncomfortable with their scrutiny and looked at them critically but saw nothing but friendliness.

A tall man, fair with long hair, waved and called in English, "we've seen your caricatures, do you draw portraits too? Us sitting on the boat it would be a nice souvenir. Do you speak English?"

Michelle smiled back, "yes certainly."

"Does that mean you certainly speak English, or you certainly will draw for us?"

Michelle laughed. "Both."

The man walked across the gangplank and offered his hand. "My name is Hans Kleiber." He was tall and lean with very blue eyes, like arctic ice she thought. He smiled and gestured to the other two men, "Karl and Pierre, my friends, Karl and I are German, Pierre is from Alsace, nearly German," he grinned.

Hans gazed appreciatively at the paintings, "You have great talent," he said inspecting the harbour scene. "I love paintings. What is it the amateur says when he wishes to appear professional. I know what I like, rather a political side step isn't it? Please," he went on, "let me help you."

He picked up the easel and pad and walked towards the boat. Michelle was about to protest, she had always made it a rule never to board the boats, preferring to work on the relative security of the quayside but Hans was across the gangplank and had set the easel down on the after deck. Michelle hesitated. After all she was only a few feet away, in the open and in full view of Andre who looked up disapprovingly. Still undecided she crossed on to the boat carrying her small collapsible stool. She looked closely at the other men, they looked harmless enough, but she took care to position herself as near to the gangplank as possible and arrange the three men across the steps leading down into the interior lounge. As she drew she studied them closely.

Karl was shorter than the others, fair like Hans, but thickset and muscular, a mass of gingery hair protruding from the neck of his t-shirt. His eyes were puffy and set close together. She would have a job with the eyes. Nose and eyes were always the key... get them right and everything was ok. She didn't like Karl much, she thought, but she wasn't there to like or dislike, they represented 500 euros. Pierre was very different, almost boyish, the darker swarthy appearance of the Latin, a studious, almost sad look in his eyes, curly black hair and a sulky mouth.

Hans and Karl chatted to her about St. Tropez and boats. The Yacht was chartered, they told her. Not too expensive when there were three involved. They were all keen windsurfers and spent their time in the deeper waters and the open areas where there were stronger winds. One always remained aboard in case of a problem. Scuba diving was Karl's other interest, harpooning fish. 'I can believe you enjoy that,' thought Michelle.

The features finished Michelle sketched in the background, typical of the harbour, she had drawn it so many times, but this time she included the setting of the boats after end.

Hans stood up and watched for a moment, "you'll have a drink?" The question was more of a statement as he reached into a portable fridge and drew out a bottle of chilled white wine. "This is good German wine, from Koblenz, which is my home," he pulled the cork and poured a liberal glass, passing it to Michelle. She didn't have the heart to refuse, besides she did so like white wine. After an appreciative swallow she stood the glass down and unclipped the finished portrait, holding it up for inspection. It was very good, she had captured the likenesses very well. She held the corner of the paper and sprayed the whole thing with hair lacquer.

"You should cover it with glass as soon as possible to avoid smudging the charcoal." She smiled.

Hans filled her glass although she protested, "you'll have me asleep in no time." Any concern she had felt was dissipated by the obvious friendliness of the man. They were harmless, just enjoying their holiday.

"Finish your drink and I will fetch your money." He picked up her easel and pad and took them back to her pitch.

Michelle relaxed and sipped her wine. Hans had disappeared into the lounge, followed by Karl.

"Do you live in Alsace Pierre?" She asked in French.

Pierre smiled, happy to speak his own language. "Not any more, I work with my father in Marseilles, he has a small yard where he repairs and charters all sorts of boats. This one..." He waved airily around, "is one of his. I look after the engines and mechanical side of things. That is why I am here really, to see that we don't break down. If we have no trouble I have a good holiday. Hans is very good to me, they are both good friends."

Hans stuck his head out of the lounge doorway and looked up at Michelle. "This is a good painting, but I don't think it is of St. Tropez, a little gaudy but by a very talented artist." Michelle could only see his head and shoulders, his face turned towards the bulkhead, obviously studying something. "Would you recognize someone else's painting?"

Michelle stood and leaned over the stairway. Hans stood aside and offered his hand for her to descend. She hesitated. She had already broken one rule by coming aboard at all. To go below would be foolhardy, but, her professional opinion had been sought, the wine had been stronger than she thought making her slightly more confident that there was nothing to fear. She carefully made her way down the five stairs taking the hand Hans offered. The light was dim after the strong evening sunshine and she blinked to adjust her eyes. On the bulkhead was a small painting. Placing one knee on the bunk she leaned over to get a better view. There was only time for her to see that the painting was nothing like St. Tropez, it was a poor, colourful print of the older part of Paris. Before she could say anything a strong muscular arm encircled her throat and she was pulled backwards, the other arm held her in a firm grip around her waist. She screamed, but the sound died in her throat as the grip tightened. Struggling made no difference, her arms and legs thrashed wildly she was pinned against her assailants body.

Terrified she fought like a wildcat, her senses screaming in terror, her mind reeling as she tried to breathe. The doors of the lounge closed quietly and she was alone with the madman who held her struggling and gasping for breath. With horror she heard the rasp

43

of the self-starter and the spluttering roar as the engines started, She gave a gigantic heave and managed to free her body from the iron grip, but before she could cry out she was swung around to face the grinning Karl, his face contorted with a sadistic grin he hit her with the flat of his hand, the blow took her across the side of the head and flung her sideways across the lounge, her body collapsing on the deck, her eyes rolled up with the pain of the blow and a sea of blackness swept over her. She lay semi-conscious, tears of terror staining her bruised face.

The Yacht cruised slowly out of the Harbour. Andre, puzzled watched it go. He hadn't seen Michelle come ashore, but then he had been across to the bar for a leak, a man has to have a leak. He had stayed for a beer. But then her gear was all there, she had obviously shot off for the same reason. He grinned and concentrated on his miniatures.

As the time went by Andre became more puzzled by Michelle's non-appearance. It wasn't like her to just up and leave. Her Honda was still parked where she had left it beside the concrete bollard. Her paintings and sketch pad were still where she had left them. As the sun settled on the horizon Andre became more convinced she had indeed left with the yacht. Not at all like Michelle, she wasn't one of those flighty ladies of the night who sought out dubious opportunities on offer along the quayside. He was sure she had not gone willingly, she loved her Brad too much for that... but then you never know. He shrugged. As darkness fell

Andre packed his gear up, uneasy about Michelle. She never stayed later than he did, always helped him pack up and stow everything, including her paintings in the small store they rented beneath the tourism office. He carried the materials across the road including Michelle's.

With a last look across the Harbour he wandered up to a burly Gendarme leaning on the side of a transport lorry, located in readiness to tow away any illegally parked car. When that happened the offending vehicle was uplifted and driven to the pound at the other end of town, its recovery costing 500 euros. Andre explained his worries about Michelle. Jules the Gendarme knew Andre and Michelle, admiring her dark beauty, but he didn't consider her any different to other frequenters of the quayside.

He listened to Andre and laughed, "Andre, mon ami, if we worried about every girl who went to sea in a boat we would all have grey hair, n'est pas."

"Michelle is not that sort Jules. She is a thoroughly decent girl. Something is wrong here very wrong. I am very worried. Anyway, I am officially reporting her to be a missing person."

"Then you must go to the Gendarmerie. I cannot take details here I am much too busy, my work is too important."

"Yeah right," said Andre sarcastically, "busy business waiting for someone to park two inches over the line, much more important than a girls' safety." The Gendarme scowled.

Andre knew he would get little help at this time of night from the local Police and decided to leave matters until the morning. Michelle was a strong girl. She could take care of herself. He tried to convince himself with no success.

Michelle opened her eyes, or tried to, a blinding pain speared through her head, she felt sick and her throat burned. She lay still, trying to collect her thoughts, her stomach knotted as everything flowed back into her mind. She was lying on a bunk, the throb of the engines firm and even. They were at sea, panic overtook her she forced her eyes open, desperately attempting to focus them. Karl sat watching her from the other side of the cabin, a large drink in his hand. He grinned at her.

"So you are back with us again, you shouldn't have struggled, "then I wouldn't have hit you."

"You bastard," Michelle croaked, her throat felt as though it was full of razor blades. She raised herself on the bunk, fighting back nausea. "What do you want, why keep me on his boat. I demand you let me off at once. I've done nothing to you pigs, any of you." She sank back, the throbbing behind her eyes easing a little.

"We only want a bit of fun," he said soothingly, "just do as we want and we won't hurt you again. We want to enjoy ourselves... you too will enjoy it if you're sensible." He swallowed his drink and lurched through the door.

Panic shuddered through her as his words sunk in. "Oh God," she cried out loud, sliding off the bunk she sat still for a moment to fight off the sick feeling and looked frantically around for a weapon of some sort. There was nothing, everything was a fixture. Screwed to the bulkhead was a hinged table top with one single leg supporting it, she gripped the leg and twisted. The leg turned, it was removable. Quickly she unscrewed it and let the top swing quietly back against the panelled partition. The feel of the solid leg in her hands gave her more confidence and quietened the shaking fear which gripped her. Quickly Michelle peered through the porthole. Sea, nothing but sea, no land, no shipping, she went to the other side the same only desolation. The boat couldn't be that far out she reasoned... What time had she come aboard? What a bloody fool she had been, no more sense than a naïve schoolgirl. How long was she out for she groaned, she had no idea. Carefully she tried the cabin door but it was locked. Cautiously she positioned herself against the bulkhead in a good position to clout the first one through the door, she waited. The door clicked and the door opened slowly. Karl stepped in and Michelle swung the leg viciously. At the last second he moved his head and the blow struck his shoulder instead of his head. He swore and ducked into the cabin, grabbing a handful of her hair as she tried to swing the club again. With a massive heave Michelle was thrown the length of the lounge. She lost her balance and stumbled against the bunk, still gripping the table leg.

"You bitch!" Snarled Karl rubbing his shoulder, his eyes were glazed with the whisky he had drunk, sour on his breath. Michelle flattened herself against the bulkhead, her eyes were flashing. "Come any nearer and I'll smash your head open," she screamed, her terror turning to a blinding hatred, "I'll kill you, I swear it." Karl hesitated, sizing Michelle up. She was a tough one he decided. He slid his hand into his pocket and a metallic click dragged Michelle's eyes to his hand. A long vicious flick-knife glinted in the dying light.

"Put that stick down or I'll slice that pretty face to ribbons," The knife flicked towards her and she went cold. He was too drunk not to mean it, the very thought of the knife terrified her. Gathering herself she leapt at him swinging the leg at his arm in desperation. She missed, drunk as he was, he had anticipated her attack and stepped aside. Off balance Michelle was grabbed by the neck and slammed face down on the bunk settee. She screamed as Karl wrenched the table leg from her hand twisting her wrist painfully. Tears of pain and frustration streamed from her eyes. "Please, please don't," she sobbed, her mental courage dissipated, her physical resistance sapped she lay sobbing all resistance gone.

Karl slung the leg across the cabin and turned her on the settee, savagely he ripped her shirt-blouse to the waist, sick and weak she felt his hands rough and lustful on her breasts. Her jeans were torn away violently. He came over her, his breath sour as his mouth crushed hers, his thrusting penetration urgent with animal insistence. Michelle drifted into a darkness of revulsion and disbelief. She hardly realized that Karl had finished with her before horror penetrating her mind Hans' puffy eyes leered at her through the haze. His mouth sought hers, her throat, her breasts, as he entered her, grunting and gasping, it seemed for ever. Mercifully Michelle lost consciousness. Time became meaningless. Michelle drifted in a sea of pain and misery, murmuring Brads name in her agony. Eventually she raised herself, sitting up on the bunk, clasping her knees, holding herself together, wishing she were dead, tears rolling down her cheeks soaking her aching thighs. The door opened and struck more terror into her, she shrunk back into the corner.

"Oh God no more, please no more." She pleaded. Pierre shook his head. "I have come to help you if I can," he said quietly, sitting on the corner of the bunk.

"Why now, why not before...?" She turned her ravaged face to him, "you could have stopped them?"

Pierre shrugged, "It was not my affair they might have killed me if I interfered." He looked disinterested.

"Why did you come aboard, you should have expected this."

"You're as bad as they are, you spineless bastard," she mouthed at him, "I'll see you in hell for this!"

Pierre stood up and left. "Cochon," muttered

Michelle.

Michelle miserably dragged her torn jean on and attempted to repair the ripped blouse, without success. She crammed the blouse into her jeans and wiped her face, flinching as she touched the bruise which spread across her cheek. The door opened. It was Hans. He peered cautiously into the room and stepped in. Michelle looked at him with hatred, uncertain.

Hans smirked. "Feeling better?"

She said nothing, fearful of another attack. Hans mistook her silence for a change of heart and stepped closer to her. Her bruised cheek took his eye.

"That looks nasty," he said putting his hand out to touch the bruise. Suddenly the whole pit of disgust, the hatred and horror of her experience erupted in Michelle from the depths of her mind and body she summoned a new strength. She leapt at Hans like a Leopard her long nails slashing his flesh, the points dug deep into his cheek, missing the eye by a fraction and ripped the flesh open from cheek bone to chin.

Blood spurted from the deep gashes and Hans screamed, staggering backwards. Michelle followed up her frenzied attack, bringing her knee up into his exposed groin sending shrieking agony through his body. Hans collapsed on the deck, his face a mass of blood, clutching his groin in an agony of pain. Frantic, Michelle, her long hair flying, eyes flashing and teeth bared dragged a pottery lamp from the bulkhead and smashed it over Hans' head as the door burst open. Karl came through the door, horrified at the shambles, Hans writhing on the deck and Michelle crouched like a beast at bay. With two steps he slammed into her crushing her face against the wooden edge of the bunk. His hairy forearm held her helpless while he looked in amazement at the bloodied Hans still groaning on the deck. Pierre left the wheel and looked in. He tried to help Hans to his feet without success the pain was too great; a deep wound had opened from the blow with the table lamp. With hatred Karl pushed angrily at Michelle's head, jamming her throat against the wooden structure. Her body went limp. Karl let her drop to the floor where she lay, an inert bundle and turned his attention to Hans. Pierre brought a damp towel and swabbed the lacerated cheek to try and staunch the flowing blood. They lifted him and lay him on the bunk.

"Christ," breathed Karl, "She's a right bitch this one, look at his face."

After a while Hans recovered, the pain subsiding. He staggered to his feet and looked in the mirror. He bellowed in horror at his image." Look at my bloody face," he sobbed, "I need stitches for Christ's sake. He aimed a vicious kick at Michelle. She had not moved. Pierre bent down and turned her on to her back. Her throat was bruised, her lips blue, eyes opening, staring. "God Almighty," He breathed, "I think she's dead." He ripped her shirt open and pressed his ear to her chest. There was no heartbeat.

"What" Hans stopped mopping his face and looked at Michelle. He felt her wrist. "No pulse." Not satisfied he pressed his face to her chest. He looked up, scared. "She's dead! You've killed her you bloody fool." He turned on Karl, fear and panic in his eyes. "What the fuck are we going to do now?"

Chapter 7

Inspector Dubois adjusted his rimless glasses and continued studying the reports spread across his desk. He sighed. There was nothing he could follow up let alone act upon. Stationed in Nice at the new Gendarmerie he had been given, carte blanche to investigate and ultimately sew up the Mafia problems in the Cote d'Azur. Just like that! The top brass were getting fidgety, crime was increasing and clear ups less frequent. Drug importation was rampant, which led to the myriad of other felonies, from murder through illegal white slavery to hundreds of other sickening activities.

He knew that Don Vittorino was behind everything. He could forgive the running of top class call girls, even street prostitution. That carried a degree of physical satisfaction which led, at worst, to divorce. C'est la vie. But the ugly side of drug use was intolerable. There was never anything concrete. He had issued instructions that every occurrence, illegal, unnatural, bizarre or abnormal be reported to him at once. Particularly wherever it happened along the coastline, hence, the pile of paper that threatened to engulf his desk. Even Paris, at its worst had nothing on this place. Everything seemed to happen here, in the most part of little consequence. Dubois was convinced the volume was an effort by his colleagues to drive him to the funny farm.

They had a good chance of succeeding. In only the last twenty four hours he had studied reports of murder, rape, drug overdoses, cat fights between homosexuals and complaints by prostitutes of attempted fraud for Christ's sake, how do you assess value for money in that case.

The door opened and a junior Gendarme entered placing a report on the desk. "Body on the beach sir," the lad said briskly, "looks like murder, young woman." He hovered expectantly.

Dubois picked up the report, "another drug overdose probably," he said. On Wednesday 15thMay at 6am the body of a young woman was discovered at the eastern end of the beach wedged into the rocks Monsieur Anton Grimad, aged 67 years of 18 Rue de la Mimosas, Cannes, discovered her as he exercised his dog and informed Police. Sergeant Claude Goy attended the scene and later arranged for the body to be taken to Cannes hospital Mortuary. Monsieur Grimaud agreed to attend the Gendarmarie later to make a statement. No identification was possible, the clothing was torn. Description, Aged approximately 28 years, dark haired, 1 metre 60 cm tall, slim build, bruising on body and throat, and a deep wound to the left forehead. Cause of death not yet established more information after post mortem. Dubois dismissed the Gendarme and set aside the report. After a few minutes he picked it up again. Bruising would indicate injury before death, possibly murder, no probably murder. He clapped his hat on his head and left the station. On arrival in Cannes he made his way to the Cannes central mortuary.

The Inspector gazed sadly at the pathetic body. She had been a beautiful woman, he thought. He examined the deep bruising of the throat and face. No doubt about the cause of death he decided. He would wait for the pathology report. The features were relaxed in death, waxen, no serious effects of the sea. She couldn't have been in the water long. Covering the body he walked away, nodding to the mortuary attendant. As he reached the door something jolted his memory. He stopped, puzzled, there was something about the girl. He turned back gesturing to the attendant to allow him to view the body again. He gazed at her face, his eyes startled, he knew her there could be no doubt. He brushed her hair back. Brad Carter, his girlfriend what was her name, Michelle, that was it Michelle le Jeune. She was that lovely creature he had met in St. Tropez. He took a deep breath.

"Dear God have mercy on us all." He turned and walked away. Why in Heavens name would anyone kill such a person? He felt a personal loss. Deeply shaken he hurried back to the office. Unwilling to be convinced that it was Michelle he sifted through his notebook and found the telephone number of her apartment. He dialled willing the phone to be answered by Michelle. The phone rang, Dubois held on, and on, there was no reply. He must obtain positive identification. The only person who could do that was Brad Carter. He thumbed through the notebook again and dialled the Paris number Brad had given him. The number was engaged.

He hung up, and turned to the pile of messages waiting for his attention, routine occurrences, he regretted his decision to have everything reported to him, but there was no other means of telling whether there was a lead or not. His eye fastened on a missing person report as he was in the act of discarding it. The name Michelle LeJeune stared at him. He read carefully.

Andre, greatly disturbed by Michelle's disappearance had gone to the Gendarmarie in St. Tropez early that morning and reported Michelle as a missing person. Correct in his assumption that the Gendarme had done nothing the desk sergeant was disinterested.

Such happenings were frequent. The girl was old enough to look after herself and make her own decisions. It was too soon to get worried. In any event Andre was no relation just a friend and told to come back in week.

Andre was furious, "your attitude will be reported to your superiors. If anything has happened to her, and I'm sure it has, woe betide your future. Dismissed no pension disgraced, all because you are too bloody idle to post her as a missing person." He turned to walk away.

"Wait," the sergeant had second thoughts and filled in all the details, albeit grudgingly. The typical French attitude of avoiding responsibility by passing the buck resulted in a telex message reaching Inspector Dubois.

Brad was just about to leave his office when the telephone jangled. He hesitated and then turned back.

"Carter," he said into the mouthpiece reaching for a cigarette.

"Inspector Dubois...!"

"What is it Inspector?" "Brad's lips pursed with annoyance. Still the bloody man plagued him. "surely you're not still chewing at the same bones?"

"It is very important M'sieu," the voice was quiet, respectful, "would it be possible for you to come to Nice at once?"

Brad was astonished whatever could be the reason to drag him all that way. "Isn't this something we could discuss on the phone?" He asked crossly. "I was hoping to come down next weekend anyway. Today is Thursday perhaps it could wait."

"I'm afraid not," replied Dubois. "I would much prefer to see you personally there are very good reasons."

His voice contained a tone which disturbed Brad. Serious, sad even. Brad looked at his watch, "couldn't you come here?" He asked hopefully, "I have a few things which need tidying up here."

"Please M'sieu Carter I would not trouble you unless it was essential. How soon do you think you could be here?"

"It's nearly noon, I could be in Nice late this afternoon I suppose, traffic willing. Where in Nice..?"

"My office is on the first floor of the new Gendarmerie," he sounded relieved, "I shall await your arrival, merci, au revoir." Dubois hung up before Brad changed his mind.

Brad lit another cigarette. The bugger must have something up his sleeve, he mused, blasted nuisance all the same time. At least he would have a few days longer with Michelle. His mood brightened at the thought. He picked up the phone and dialled Michelle. No reply. No doubt at work or too lazy to get up. He grinned and locked his office. Stopping only to buy a beer and sandwich he drove belligerently through the lunchtime traffic and headed for the Paris-Lyon Autoroute.

Dubois toyed with thought of immediately following up the Missing Persons report. He didn't know the informant... Andre L'essin, chances were that he wouldn't be at the address in Croix Valmer, better leave it until Carter arrived. It was too far to be sure of getting back to Nice in time. Besides there was a possibility he was mistaken. He knew that he was not. Brad arrived at 6pm. Stiff from the drive, hot and sticky and dying for a shower. Better be worth it he thought as he was shown into Dubois office. Dubois ordered coffee, seemingly unwilling to broach the subject. Why does life contain so much sadness? He wished he had been a gardener or something similar.

"Now Inspector, what's all this about, it had better be important. I offered to help if I could," Brad shrugged, "nothing more has happened as far as I know."

Slowly and quietly Dubois spoke to Brad. The finding of the body, his recognition in the mortuary the missing persons report, the unanswered telephone calls, need for identification, authority for an autopsy...

Brad sat transfixed, his eyes staring with disbelief. The blood had drained from his face and fear flooded through his body gripping his chest in an iron band. He felt as if he were turned to stone, fists clenched, the nails biting into his palms, unnoticed, unfelt. One word penetrated his shattered mind, identification...

"You are not sure then?" The words seem to come from a long way away. It seemed his was above the scene, watching, not part of this nightmare. He refused to be part of this mad horror.

"Not absolutely..." Dubois was careful not to inject too much indecision the shock must be once and once only, no slight raising of the hopes then a second slam into the abyss.

"Where is she...?" A small light flickered in his desperate eyes.

"Cannes hospital, I'll take you there now if you can manage it. Perhaps you should see a Doctor. Rest a while this is a terrible thing for you to bear." He lit a cigarette for Brad.

The ride to the hospital was silent. Brad sat rigid his mind struggling to accept the impossible. Another girl... they all looked so similar these days. Dubois didn't really know Michelle, in death features changed. No-one could want to hurt Michele, not his Michelle, his wonderful Michelle. Oh God don't let it be her! As the attendant turned back the crisp sheet, Brad knew it was her. He gazed, his face expressionless, at the bruised features, the closed eyes that danced like sunlight, her mouth, that lovely smiling mouth which had caressed him. He leaned over and kissed her slate cold face. He turned away, unaware of anyone or anything, his mind frozen with deep shock, his movements automatic his eyes unseeing. Dubois hurried after him and took his arm. There was no need to ask the reaction in Brad was enough.

At the Gendarmarie Brad walked towards his car. The Inspector protested. "You should not drive M'sieu. Please come into the Station for a while, some coffee a drink, time to recover, to think." Dubois was worried he had never seen a reaction to tragedy such as this.

"I am all right Inspector," Brad turned to him, face ashen, rigid. "I must be on my own, I cannot help, but I will be in touch." He climbed into the BMW, and drove slowly out of the car park.

Dubois signalled to a police car, engine idling parked outside the main building. He leaned into the driver's door. "Follow that car, discreetly, do not interfere with him in any way whatever he does. I am concerned for his safety that is all." The driver started to argue. "Do as I say," Dubois snapped, "telephone me when he reaches his destination."

The car drove off, the driver muttering obscenities under his breath. The drive was something Brad would never remember, an automatic reaction controlled by his subconscious mind. He could not think, his mind a flickering kaleidoscope of meaningless fragments, deep shock enveloping and saving his mind from total madness.

He let himself into the apartment at St. Tropez, leaning back on the door as he closed it, the familiar tang of polish and perfume pervading his nostrils. He walked into the lounge it was quiet, oppressively quiet, resentful in its desolation. He sat down staring at the floor, seeing nothing. Later he rose and walked slowly through the rooms, the bedroom, Michelle's t-shirts draped over the chair, he straightened a pillow absently, the lounge neat and tidy. His eyes went to the bureau, a photograph of Michelle and himself taken at Cannes a year ago, smiled back at him. There was a small vase holding a bunch of brilliant violets in front of the photo. Michelle changed the flowers regularly. While the flowers lived their love would never die.' She had said. It was the flowers that finally broke his heart. He pulled them from the vase and held them close to him.

A deep wracking sob churned through his body, bursting into streaming acidic tears flooding unchecked. He cried for Michelle, for himself, for their love, he cried with the frustration of helplessness, the loneliness and the sheer savage waste of something beautiful which now could never be. He cried deep into the night, holding in final desperation to the pillow which held the lingering nearness of Michelle. He cried until he was totally drained and exhausted, physically and mentally, and drifted into a fog of unconsciousness.

PART TWO
Chapter 8

Later the next morning Brad roused, hurting, his eyes sunken and dark his body tender and cold. The pain and misery has dissipated a little and a new emotion had awakened an oily pervading sickness deep in his gut. He recognized it as hatred, a deep, all enveloping hatred of whoever was responsible for the brutal death of Michelle. He showered, willing the hot streaming jets to renovate his shattered thinking. Andre knew something. He would go and find Andre. They had met a few times in the past, he was a sound character. He would help. He swallowed a steaming cup of coffee and dressed quickly, hoping the leaden ball of violence would disappear from his stomach. It did not.

As Brad arrived, Andre was busy setting up his paraphernalia alongside the quay. He was surprised and delighted to see Brad and shook his hand with great warmth, but was concerned with the haggard face and sunken eyes.

"You have news of Michelle?" Careful to avoid too much concern before knowing that Brad knew she had disappeared.

"Michelle is dead Andre, murdered, found in the sea, washed up near Cannes." Brad spoke quietly his voice devoid of expression, not allowing himself to slip back into the darkness.

Andre's mouth fell open and tears fell from his startled eyes, "Michelle dead, mon Dieu." He crossed himself.

"You reported her missing Andre, why, what happened to make you do that?"

Andre, eyes brimming recounted what had happened, "she never went aboard these boats, Brad, "he said sadly, "just this one time. When I returned the boat had gone, I thought she had come ashore and gone for a drink or something. I didn't realize," he concluded lamely.

"What boat Andre?" Brad was shaken, Dubois had said nothing of any boat, perhaps he didn't yet know.

"I don't know there are so many. This one was tied up for almost a week, went out daily and returned in the evenings. There were three men aboard, German I think. German flag, I couldn't see the name it was too near the wall. I think it was out of Marseilles." Andre brightened. "The Marine Office would know. They must have booked the mooring."

"Where's that, the Marine Office?"

"Next to the Abbate boat yard, come I will show you." Andre led the way stepping carefully through the debris of ropes and boxes, past the market to a small office tucked into the rambling row of buildings. A Customs Officer sat behind a cluttered desk poring over a newspaper, pencil poised. He looked up as the men entered.

"Oui." He looked annoyed at being disturbed.

Brad asked him if he knew the owners of the boat which had occupied berth 5a for the past week or so.

"What is the name of the boat?"

"I don't know. I was hoping you would have that information."

The man pursed his lips, another stupid enquiry, nosey bloody tourist they think every boat is owned by a film star.

"Without a name I can do nothing." he bent over his newspaper.

Andre leaned across the desk and gently removed the pencil from his hand. The man looked puzzled. Holding the pencil between his fingers Andre suddenly snapped it in half. The man jumped and sat up quickly.

"If you take the trouble to look I'm sure you will be able to tell us what we need to know mon ami n'est pas." His French was heavy with the local dialect and threatening undertones.

The Customs Office thought better of tangling with this hairy and brawny hippie, he searched through his files.

"The motor Yacht, "Pandora," owned by a boat yard in Marseilles, chartered for 2 weeks by Mr Hans Kleiber.

Fees paid up to the 20th."

"Anything else…?" He asked with heavy sarcasm.

"Address of Hans Kleiber…"

"Not known, none of our business, you'll have to ask the owners."

"And they are?"

The man looked at the file. "Pegasus, Marseilles." He slammed the drawer shut.

They walked out.

"Let's have a beer and talk," suggested Andre, "I would like to help, if I can, Michelle was such a lovely person. I loved her, in my own way."

In the bar Brad decided to ring Dubois. He was undecided whether to tell him what he had learnt, but he wanted more information.

Dubois answered the phone and was relieved to hear Brad was recovering. "I have results of the Post Mortem now M'sieu Carter if you wish to know. The findings are not pleasant."

"Tell me," Brad braced himself.

"The cause of death has been established as being asphyxiation, from pressure exerted across the throat by a hard object. She would have been dead before being thrown into the sea, there was no water in the lungs. There were extensive injuries, primarily bruising across the left side of the face and a more severe blow to the head. With abrasions and bruising of the body..."

"What else?" Brad asked grimly sensing hesitation by Dubois.

"She had been raped," his voice was embarrassed, unwilling to cause more distress. Brad swallowed hard. "A number of times, a vicious sexual attack a great deal of internal injury. Her finger nails disclosed a significant amount of torn flesh. She caused some deep wounds on her attackers face, enough for our forensics to obtain a clear DNA of her attacker. This will be crucial evidence when we find him or them. The poor soul put up a strenuous fight for her life."

Brad took a deep breath, "when you find them. What happens then Inspector, I'll tell you. They will be charged with murder, find a clever attorney and plead Not Guilty. Their evidence will be that the girl was a willing victim that they were drunk, that she changed her mind because of the drink, that there was no murder, they had not meant to kill her, it was an unfortunate accident. They panicked and are dreadfully sorry. I don't think so Inspector."

"M'sieu Carter...!" Dubois was alarmed by the venom in Brads' voice. "I assure you that the full force of the law will deal adequately with this crime. He, or they, will get life imprisonment and be interned in a French jail, which is not a pleasant experience. It is important that we meet, and I speak with the man who first reported her missing. There may be others who saw something. Believe me the Law will ensure Justice will be done."

"There is only one Justice in this case," said Brad bitterly, "the good book makes that clear. An eye for an eye...'

"Please M'sieu I urge you not to pursue on your own, you could well come to harm and also fall foul of the Law yourself. Leave it to me."

"Thank you Inspector. I shall be in touch! Brad hung up.

Dubois bit his lip, frowning.

"They raped her Andre." Brad returned to the bar and sat down. "Raped her and hurt her, then they killed her and threw her over the side."

Andre shuddered. "God have mercy." he breathed.

"God may, if he wishes, but I certainly shan't." He managed to shut the misery from his mind, he must think straight, must find these animals, smash them, kill them, for Michelle, for himself, but how, who were they, where were they. His only lead was the boatyard in Marseilles they would know this Kleiber.

"I must go to Marseilles. "He raised his eyes to Andre, "to find Kleiber."

Andre shook his head dubiously. "I know how you feel Brad, but Marseilles is no place for you. It is full of worthless scum, the dregs, if you ask too many questions, especially as you are not French, you could get into a very dangerous situation. These men have already killed they will not stop to kill again. Let the Police handle it," his tone was persuasive, "they will find Kleiber and the others, don't put yourself in danger, Michelle would not want you to do that."

Brad smiled sadly at Andre, squeezing his shoulder. "Thank you for your concern my friend, but I must do it my way. My life and safety are no longer of any importance. What is important is that I must even the score. Without you I would have nothing to go on, but now I have the name of one bastard and at least a chance of finding him."

Andre shrugged resignedly, there was no point in arguing, "let me come with you. I speak their language, I understand the French, can sense things." He looked at Brad hopefully.

"Perhaps," nodded Brad, "But you have your work here."

Andre grinned, "you see, you know nothing about the French, we only need the slightest excuse to avoid work and we can be lazier than anyone. Come I have Michelle's things in the storeroom, you will want them, there are many good paintings so much like Michelle, colourful, sincere, beautiful."

Brad loaded the gear into the back of his car, the chill seeping through his chest as he handled the paintings; he laid them carefully on the back seat, the easel in the boot the sketch pad smooth and white on the top. Andre agreed to look after the Honda. He drove away promising to speak with Andre again before he did anything. Back at the apartment Brad phoned Dubois again as he had promised.

Inspector Dubois was relieved. He was becoming frustrated by the lack of progress into what was a very brutal murder with nothing much to work on, plus the continual pressure for him to get some movement in the drug problems. His sixth sense told him that Brad knew more than he was admitting. He arranged for them to meet in St. Tropez the next morning, not sure that he would agree to come to Nice.

"I shall be there at 10am, please do nothing until we have talked, there are things to discuss, including the inquest you understand."

Sharp at 10am he arrived with a leather briefcase, polished and immaculate as he was. As Brad made coffee, he decided to tell Dubois as little as possible, only the facts that he could find out for himself. He related the discussion he had with Andre, whom he said had seen nothing apart from Michelle sketching the three men on board. He had left and was unaware whether Michelle had left the boat or not. More than that, he'd done nothing as Dubois had requested. Dubois looked at Brad, unsure.

"This morning I received the report from the pathologist, following the P.M." He pulled out a sheet of heavily embossed paper from his briefcase. "It was noted that the flesh beneath her nails was of a male facial flesh as I told you on the phone, deep scratches which will result in scarring. We are looking for someone with such an injury, the first real evidence to come to light." Dubois smiled with satisfaction. "The facts are, and I repeat, facts are that a young woman, whom we now know to be Mamselle LeJeune was found, washed up from the sea after approximately 26 hours of immersion. Prior to this she was last seen in the proximity of a motor launch, details unknown, on the quayside at St. Tropez. As yet there has been no official decision as to how she met her death that is the prerogative of the Coroner, although, of course we know that she was brutally murdered."

Brad was getting sick to death of the officious and pompous attitude and speech by Dubois. By now the whole Gendarmerie should be swarming like bees, seeking, searching, investigating, pulling out all the stops to locate these mindless swine, not sitting here pontificating like a bloody vicar giving a sermon!

"Quite honestly Inspector you are beginning to make me sick! You are not dealing with an abstract problem, you are, or should be, investigating the brutal murder of a lovely young woman who never did an unloving thing in her life. She brought nothing but happiness and beauty into this life and you burble on about correct procedures, evidence, facts. What more facts do you need? Three sadistic animals abduct the girl, rape her, kill her and throw her overboard like a bag of garbage. For Christ's sake get yourself and your moronic team off their butts and find these bastards. Or I will." He finished ominously.

Dubois, shaken by the intensity of the outburst, was at a loss.

"I must caution you against taking any steps..."

"Fuck your cautions Dubois, and Fuck you too!"

Affronted Dubois rose to his feet. "I can sympathise with your feelings Monsieur Carter, but not your attitude. There is no need for such language. Please be at the Inquest at 10am on Wednesday." He passed an official form to Brad and marched out.

Brad caught him at the front door. "Sorry Inspector."

Dubois looked at Brad and smiled. "Je comprend," he said.

The Inquest was routine. A verdict of death from unnatural causes, and that appeared to be the end of it. The clerk of the Coroners Court asked Brad if he would like the personal property found on Michelle.

"What was there?" Asked Brad...

"Only her jeans and a shirt no jewellery, nothing else..."

Brad, puzzled, shook his head. He could never remember Michelle without something in the jewellery line on her wrists or fingers. Michelle was buried in the small churchyard, in front of the Church of Santa Maria. The Church had been built to accommodate about 40 worshippers. There were over a hundred, who filled the Church and spilled out across the paths and grass. The grave overlooked the Bay and the sea which rippled gently. Dubois was there and almost all the traders from the Market which had closed in deference to the loss of one of their favourite people. Her coffin was white and smothered in flowers as it was carried to the graveside. The ancient organ played her favourite hymn, 'All things bright and beautiful,' to the best of its ability.

Earlier Brad had looked upon her for the last time. He kissed her face and slipped an engagement ring on to her finger. He had intended to propose at the weekend. He placed a single red rose in her hand. As the coffin was lowered gently flowers were thrown on to it from all directions. After the priest had said his piece the crowds moved away and Brad was left standing alone. He felt he had died too.

Andre rescued him. "Come mon ami, together we get drunk....very drunk."

Chapter 9

On board the Pandora the three men were worried and frightened. In the immediate panic of finding Michelle dead, they'd unceremoniously dumped her body overboard into the darkness of the open sea. After checking that there was no means of identification, it was then they decided to return the boat to Marseilles. The Charter time was nearly up anyway. They would then go their own ways and say nothing.

"If you are asked any questions Pierre, you know nothing, right." Hans, his scarred face still bleeding turned his ice cold eyes on the younger man. "If anyone saw her come aboard to do the sketch, you agree that she did, but she left again before we sailed, you understand?"

Pierre was scared, "Yes, of course, but who will ask questions. No-one knows the boat, no-one knows us."

"I booked the bloody mooring didn't I," Hans snarled, "they have my name and the boatyard belongs to your father. If anyone comes snooping around it will be there."

"I must warn my father then," said Pierre, "he must know to say nothing, anyone asking questions will go straight to him. I am never in the office only in the Yard."

Karl swore. "No one must know what happened, otherwise it will all come out," his puffy eyes mirrored his fear, "It was an accident anyway, I didn't mean to kill her, just stop her she was crazy."

Hans sneered. "You got plenty of guts knocking women about, but none when the shit hits the fan. If you tell your father Pierre he will go straight to the Police." Hans mopped his face.

"No," said Pierre, "he will protect me. I had nothing to do with it, he wouldn't want me involved."

"You're just as involved as we are," shouted Hans, "standing by and doing nothing is as bad as doing it yourself."

"I didn't rape her. I didn't lay a hand on her. I couldn't have stopped you anyway."

"I didn't notice you trying either," Karl growled.

It was decided to return the boat and that Pierre should tell his father that there had been an accident with the girl, who was a willing guest. She was pushed over the side in panic. They sailed on towards Marseilles. At 8am they rounded the point and motored slowly through, Avant Port Sud, past the customs and carefully turned into the 'Bassin de Lazeret. The Pegasus Boatyard lay beneath the gaze of the Cathedral, the jetty was almost full, boats of all shapes and sizes were high and dry inside the rusting gates. They secured the boat and tramped into the yard, their packed cases weighing them down. Pierre and Hans climbed the stairs to the main Office, and opened the door.

A young brash blonde girl sat at the desk, eyebrows plucked to a thin arch, her breasts bulging though a flimsy t-shirt, her skirt short and high on her thighs. She smiled at Pierre and pushed her heavily made up face towards him for a perfunctory kiss. Her eyes rested for a moment on the scarred face of Hans which he was trying to conceal with a bloodied handkerchief.

"You're back early," she said, brightly, "not due for a couple of days yet, any problems?"

"None," said Pierre, "Hans has to be back at work soon, he hurt his face, fell on the stairway."

The girl looked concerned and made to examine Hans' face. He pulled away angrily. "It is nothing," he muttered.

Yvonne shrugged, probably pissed, she thought, not that I'm worried about his damned face as long as he doesn't shout about compensation.' She sat down, showing an ample amount of leg. She pushed a ledger across the desk thumbing back a few pages.

"Sign here, everything is paid, as long as there is no damage." She raised an eyebrow at Pierre.

"No she's fine, still afloat." Hans signed against the entry, shook Pierre's hand and nodded to Yvonne. He turned and walked out of the office, "See you around."

"Surly sod," said Yvonne, poking her tongue out at

the closed door.

"Dad in...?" Pierre asked.

Yvonne laughed. "You've got to be joking, it's not 9 yet, you know he never shows up before eleven." She got up to make some coffee from a small machine in the corner. Want a cup?"

Pierre nodded and sat down glumly, worrying about his father, worrying about the whole damned business. Hans and Karl left the yard and walked to the long term car park. They climbed into a black Sirocco and drove away. Hans dropped Karl at the Gare due Prado, the railway station serving the North West, Karl was returning to Nimes, as was Hans. They parted, Hans not offering to give Karl a lift. Hope I never see the bastard again,' thought Hans as he drove off.

Chapter 10

Brad drove to Marseilles deciding not to tell Andre, he didn't want to involve the friendly and contented frenchman in his plans, things were too precarious at this stage. The huge city sprawled in all directions the outskirts criss–crossed with ring roads and autoroute signs. He followed signs to the port. The traffic was heavy and frustrating, numerous traffic lights delayed him, the baleful red light glowing at the impatient traffic which was nose to tail along the Rue de Rome. Horns blared incessantly, french drivers firmly believing that the harder they leaned on their horns, the quicker the gridlock would disappear. He turned at the massive junction towards Vieux Port in the older part of the docks and slowed. He had little to go by. The telephone directory merely gave the address of the Pegasus Boat Yard as the Place de la Jolliette. He asked a swarthy seaman and was answered with a disinterested shrug. The Hotel de Ville, the Town Hall, came into view and Brad pulled into a parking bay. A Gendarme stood at the entrance, Brad asked for directions. He was pleased to find the yard was within walking distance. He locked the car and set off. The smell of fish pervaded the heavy air. It was lunchtime and the love of the French for their buoillebase fish stew added to the atmosphere. Finally he saw a faded sign, 'Chantier Pegasus with an arrow pointing forlornly to nothing, the word bureau, small beneath it, Brad entered the cluttered yard. the noise of a sanding machine shrill in his ears, he ducked under a large ocean going yacht looking sad and naked with most of the peeling paint sanded away. Another sign indicated a flight of wooden stairs. As he entered Yvonne sat up with interest, she smiled, he was nice, a cut above the usual tatty lot.

"What can I do for you?" She asked, thinking of many things they could do together. Brad looked at her noticing the books and papers cluttering the desk.

"Some information if you would please."

"Of course," Yvonne responded immediately, "is it for boat repair?" He looked as if he owned a boat, "hire or charter?"

"Just information, you own a boat named, 'Pandora' I believe?"

Yvonne's face went hard, her eyes narrowed. "Yes," she said cautiously. Brad didn't miss her change of expression. He had hit a nerve already.

"Could you tell me who has her on charter at present? I see the boat is here."

Yvonne nodded her head, very cautious now. She looked at Brad stonily.

"Who has her on charter?" Brad persisted. "I believe it could be a Mr. Hans Kleiber?"

She was obviously very worried now and nervous. "I can't give you any information about our clients, M'sieu.

You must ask my boss. Such information is confidential M'sieu Falaise is not," her voice trailed off as the door of the inner office opened, a short fat man, dressed in ill-fitting slacks and a colourful shirt, open almost to the waist, peered at Brad over half-moon spectacles. He was around forty, his hair thin on top and unwashed.

"M'sieu was asking about the Pandora, I told him he should speak with you."

Warily Falaise took a half smoked cigar from his mouth and spat out a piece of tobacco. "You'd better come in." He turned and walked into the office. Surprisingly the office was well fitted and expensive, thick piled carpet and a gleaming mahogany desk dominated the room. The windows were shaded against the sunlight by coloured venetian blinds. The whole office exuded opulence. Must be dough in the boat business, thought Brad.

"What do you want?" Falaise asked belligerently, flicking a lighter and drawing on the cigar stub. His eyes didn't leave Brads face, piggy eyes, suspicious and distrustful.

"I'm looking for Hans Kleiber, he chartered the Pandora recently. Where can I find him?"

"Who the hell are you, a bloody 'Flic?"

"No I'm not the police but I need to speak with him."

Falaise eased his bulk into the swivel chair behind the desk, without offering Brad a seat. "Don't know him, could have been the last charter, have to check. Why do you need to meet him?"

"Many reasons," replied Brad quietly, "where can I find him?"

"Don't know that it's any of your fucking business! Who the hell are you, to come barging into my office demanding information about my clients. I would soon be out of business if I did that." The last words were as offensive as he could make them.

"Perhaps the Police would be interested." Brad tried a shot in the dark. It didn't work.

"Send in the bloody army if you want to!" Falaise got up angrily, "this is a legitimate organization. I have nothing to hide from anyone. Now get out and don't come here again with your threats or i'll heave you into the docks."

Brad doubted the legitimacy of the organization, but not the violence in the man. Obviously he would get nowhere. He left, Yvonne's eyes following him curiously. At the door he hesitated and took his business card from his pocket and handed it to her. "If you hear anything, please ring me."

The door slammed behind him.

"I told you," Andre threw his arms up in despair. "Why didn't you let me come, you're lucky you didn't get a knife in your ribs. "Oh la la, you will get into big trouble if you go on like this. Now Kleiber will know you are looking for him and will be on the alert." Andre looked so woebegone that Brad had to laugh.

"It's bad enough you going for me," he said, "if Dubois finds out he'll probably slap me in the Bastille."

"At least you'd be safe there," commented Andre drily. "He came to see me an hour ago. I only told him what you said, not that I know much more, leave it to the police Brad, they'll find Kleiber and the others, don't take any more risks."

"Perhaps you're right." Brad rubbed his eyes wearily, sick with disappointment and frustration. "I'll join you tomorrow we can have a drink together." Andre looked happy at that, satisfied that the heat had gone out of Brad. "We can get drunk, very drunk. It doesn't help but it is great fun trying." Brad grinned and drove away.

At the apartment, Brad busied himself sorting out a little of Michelle's things, but soon lost heart. It was too painful yet. There was no-one to contact that he knew of, Michelle's parents had died in a boating accident years ago, the sea now had claimed her as well, he thought grimly. The light was fading, Brad switched on the light, he gathered up the paintings collected from Andre and stacked them carefully in a corner of the bedroom. The white sketch pad he dropped on the bed. If only you could talk, he muttered, but the virgin whiteness stared blankly. He walked out of the bedroom, about to switch off the light when he stopped, puzzled the pad wasn't completely blank, something had flickered as he dropped it. He picked up the pad and looked closely. There was nothing there, he tilted the paper... there was something the electric light had caught the sheen of indentations. Eagerly he turned the sheet this way and that. It was impossible to make out anything clearly but there were indentations on the sheet. Carefully he detached the sheet and rolled it into a tube. A shimmer of excitement surged through him, perhaps the sheet could talk. Perhaps the images of the murdering swine were imprinted on the second sheet. How the hell could he find out? His spirits drooped, he poured a drink perhaps graphite sprinkled across the page and puffed away would reveal any images, as can happen with fingerprints. There must be a better way. With a sudden impulse he searched through his cell phone address list and found the number he wanted. Greg Little if ever a man was misnamed, it was he. Built like a bomb shelter, he had been a colleague and friend for years while they worked for 'Paris Match.' Greg had left the paper and taken a job with 'Nice Matin' after marrying one of the models he had been sent to interview. If anyone would have some ideas, it would be Greg. Brad dialled… Brigitte answered. It had been months since he last saw them both, but she greeted him as if it were only the day before.

"Brad darling, how lovely how are you? When are you coming to see us?" Her voice was warm and comforting, Brad didn't realize how lonely he was.

"That's why I phoned Brigitte. I'd love to see you both again, and I have something to ask Greg about."

"Right," said Brigitte practically, "I'll fetch him and you can arrange it with him, if the big lump is awake.

He's watching telly, hang on."

Gregs voice boomed through the phone, the American accent still strong and full of warmth. "Hi pal…Long time no see, has she been sleeping on your shirt tails again?"

"Good to hear you Greg, I need to talk with you." Brad was suddenly aware of how badly he needed someone. Greg caught a little of the desperation in Brads, voice, his banter dropped, "Is all well buddy?" He asked anxiously.

"Can I come over Greg?" he ignored the question," I know it's late but it's important."

"Of course you can, stay as long as you like. I can never get this broad of mine into bed before I'm tired out. It's a new system, the liberated woman has to wear you out so you drop straight off, taken the place of the headache. Bring that delicious Michelle too. I might do a part exchange, cash adjustment of course."

"I'll be there in an hour," said Brad, anxious to avoid details on the phone. He hung up.

Brad arrived at Greg's home under the hour. It was a three storey four bedroomed fisherman's cottage, built alongside one of the canals in Port Grimaud. The canals wove their way throughout the port, each property with its own mooring cleverly angled to catch the sun most of the day. The canals were crammed with yachts of all shapes and sizes, most of them rarely going to sea, multi-million pounds of luxury owned by a mass of multi-millionaires and celebrities.

Greg and Brigitte had one child, Gabrielle, now three and a half going on eighteen! A small and delicate daughter with the finely chiselled features of her mother and the beauty which had made her mother a super model, this coupled with the mischief of Greg made her a sheer delight. She was sound asleep.

Greg opened the door to Brad and grabbed him by the shoulders. "Gee it's good to see you buddy, where's that gorgeous Michelle?"

"No Michelle," said Brad and hugged Brigitte fondly.

Greg looked intently at Brad, 'Christ the old boy looks old, tired out, something's wrong he decided. He looked at Brigitte, her arm around Brads' waist, looking concerned. Indoors Brad sank into an easy chair.

"Michelle is dead." He looked up at two startled faces, "raped, murdered and thrown off a boat. She was washed up at Cannes a few days ago."

"Oh my God!" Brigitte cried. "Not Michelle, not lovely Michelle."

Greg could not speak his mind was shocked as he sank into his chair, "Jesus Christ!" He swore.

Brigitte recovered first from the initial shock. Her female mind assessed the situation swiftly and accurately, Brad was on the verge of a serious collapse, the thin brittle cocoon of self-preservation he had spun would split if he was required, at that moment, to relate any details.

"Practicality darling..." Her mothers' voice rang in her memory, "In a crisis do something practical, it will save the day, save your screaming like a gibbering idiot for later the only answer in a crisis is practicality."

"When did you last eat Brad?" Brigitte looked fondly into his haggard face. The unexpectedness of the question startled him, he suddenly realised he was starving. "I don't really know, can't remember."

"Right," Brigitte marched off into the kitchen. "No more questions, no more explanations until you've eaten."

Greg was still in shock, "Goddamn! Goddamn it to hell."

"Greg," called Brigitte, "pour us a drink, large one's for me for Gods' sake."

She bared white even teeth at him as he started to say something. He got the message. Brad flicked his eyes in gratitude to her. In what seemed only a moment a steaming omelette appeared in front of Brad, salad and a basket of bread. Brigitte apologised for the bread. "French bread is born prematurely, full of life one minute, turn around and its stone dead." Brigitte covered her mouth regretting her words. Brad ate hungrily, thank God for these two he thought, relaxing his fragmented mind, shifting back to sanity.

Brigitte felt a rush of emotions, an icy band clutching at her insides she was desperate to know what had happened, most of all why? Michelle of all people, practicality, she washed the dishes with unnecessary vigour, waiting for the right moment.

Brad told them everything, quietly, without emotion, Brigitte, biting back her tears and anguish, Greg, swallowing hard, his eyes awash...

"So I rang you it seems I need some help."

Greg pulled himself together, "You'll get more help than Fort Knox has gold," he smiled, his heart going out to Brad, feeling the same hatred for those responsible.

"But not tonight," said Brigitte firmly, it's nearly 2 am and Brad is tired out."

He was despatched to the main bedroom, supplied with a massive pair of Greg's pyjamas. He slid into crisp, cool sheets with relief and drifted immediately into the first deep sleep he had experienced since the whole nightmare began.

Chapter 11

Brad rose late, feeling better, fitter, more able to cope, the slimy worm of hatred still present but he was able to push that aside and think straight. Greg was busy on the phone, pumping colleagues for more information. He explained to his Editor that he would be busy for a few days. Brigitte fussed around Brad, serving breakfast, making sure little Gabrielle behaved herself. She had thrown her pudgy arms around Brads' neck and kissed him, delighted to see him she wriggled on his lap chattering incessantly.

"She never shuts up," Greg grinned, "but of course she has the finest tutor of all time." Brigitte stuck her tongue out in a very unladylike gesture.

Brad produced the sheet of paper from Michelle's pad and carefully spread it across the table. They all peered at it closely, the indentations faint, but unmistakable. Greg looked dubious.

"There's nothing very clear here is there," he muttered, "I suppose we might be able to photograph it if we sprinkle it with graphire."

"I wondered if your office has a means of enlargement, increasing clarity, something like that, they're always printing masses of photographs in the Nice Martin, they must have some up to date equipment?"

"What about Moshe?" Brigitte called from the bathroom, busily soaping Gabrielle.

"Moshe...?" Greg looked blank.

"Moshe, from the hospital, he's always messing about with cameras and stuff. He might know what could be done."

Greg's face lit up. "Of course, just the guy, he's a nut," he offered by way of explanation to Brad.

"He's sweet," Brigitte added, Gabrielle squealing as water poured over her. "ok... a sweet nut." Greg picked up the phone and dialled.

"He might be at work, does a lot of jiggery-pokery from home though," he mused as the line connected. He works at Frejus hospital radiography, lasers all that crap."

"Moshe...?"

"Who else would it be?"

"Bon jour mon ami. Ca va. C'est moi Greg..."

"Bon jour Greg. How can I help?"

"I have a problem for you. Can I come to see you?" Greg's French was fluent and fast.

"I don't have problems....just solutions."

Greg spoke for some minutes, outlining the reason for the call. "I'll pay you of course."

"You are kind, there is only one alternative to money, poverty!" He hung up.

"He's at home, lives just north of Frejus If we go straight there he'll look at the paper, doesn't hold much hope, but he'll try. Why do Jewish people always answer a question with another fucking question?"

"Language...!" Brigitte was still in the bathroom.

Moshe lived in a converted farmhouse. The main room had been converted into a total living area, a large and ancient bed huddled in one corner, a large pine table, built to last beyond eternity dominated the room, cluttered with magazines and newspapers. A huge dresser groaned under the weight of books, crockery and a magnificent TV and hi fi, totally out of character with the rest of the place. Moshe showed them in and threw an armful of clothing on to the bed, making room on a battered settee for Greg and Brad to sit. He was a spindly youth, tall, in his early twenties, a mass of unruly hair tumbling over his large ears. His thin, birdlike features were dominated by huge, tinted spectacles which intrigued Brad. They seemed to have a life of their own, sliding down a long thin nose as he spoke, only to be shoved back with a practiced gesture after they completed their journey. He listened gravely to the basic facts, and took the roll, without unrolling it, opened a door and walked through. Greg and Brad followed and were astonished. In complete contrast to the living room this was a place of neat efficiency, walls and ceilings were black, shelves surrounding the room were stacked with equipment both, intact or dismantled. Stood in one corner a stack of snow white boards relieved the blackness. Overhead, beneath the one central light was a metal beam supporting a row of multi-coloured lights, each one on an adjustable swivel arm. Moshe carefully unrolled the paper and clipped the corners firmly to a shiny plastic table directly below the lights. He peered at the lights and drew down a blue ultra violet spot light. He switched it on and positioned it so the light spread obliquely across the table. The indentations stood out as though they were alight themselves. Nothing was recognizable as features. There were gaps and completely blank areas, but Moshe nodded gravely.

"It might work, after all." He said, the spectacles starting on their journey.

"What might?" Greg was excited.

"I will explain," Moshe slid the specs back up his nose. "There is a relatively new procedure in surgical medicine." Moshe leaned on the table, peering at his long sensitive fingers. "Called Heat Scanning, pressure exerted on, or in the body, head, lungs, stomach by a foreign body, such as a cyst or tumour causes inflammation, just the same as a stay in the eye. Inflammation means heat, internally as well as externally. It is now possible to photograph heat and accurately locate the site of the problem, invaluable in brain surgery." Moshe looked up profoundly his spectacles on the tip of his nose. Brad felt like pushing them up for him.

"How does that help," Brad asked, "there is no heat present in that piece of paper."

Moshe looked at him sadly. "Indeed there is, pressure means heat, bend a piece of wire to and fro see how hot it gets. I have developed a camera which works in much the same way as heat scanning. I am interested in metal fatigue. Checks for metal fatigue are lengthy and costly. My camera records stress in metal as soon as it starts, cheaper than taking a photograph instead of grounding an aircraft for lengthy chemical analysis."

"It works?" Greg sounded incredulous.

"Very well," Moshe nodded. To Brads' relief the spectacles returned to the starting gate.

"Will it work on paper, that's not quite like a bloody Jumbo Jet?"

"I don't know," Moshe shrugged, "I'll try."

Moshe searched in the dresser and finally located a bottle of red wine, the label peeling and the Supermarket sticker still obvious. He pulled the cork and sniffed the contents, "should be ok." He rinsed two glasses and placed them on the table. "I won't be long, can't have you in there." he nodded to the other room, "secret stuff you understand. I know what you newspaper people are." He grinned. He disappeared into the workshop closing the door firmly.

Brad looked at Greg, "some nut," he said.

Greg poured the wine suspiciously as though it was some sort of witches brew. "I didn't say he wasn't a clever nut."

Almost an hour later Moshe emerged, a wad of paper in his hand. He no longer wore his spectacles. Calmly he laid the sheets in front of Brad. Brad looked, disappointment his first re-action. The sheet was covered in a pattern of lines, some darker than others with varying blotches of light and darker areas.

"Looks like a psychiatrists' notebook to me." Greg said irreverently. Moshe looked offended.

"It is very clear, when you connect visually," he said. "The English Sunday papers, years ago, published a photograph taken from an aircraft flying over the Alps. It was a picture that looked like the face of Christ, made up of snow and dark shadows. Half the readers saw it immediately, the others never did, it's just the way you look at it. Narrow your eyes look through the picture, not at it, look at it differently. All things considered it is a good likeness of each man."

Try as they may they made no sense of the picture, but, at least, the reproduction was clear and more substantial that the faint indentations. They thanked Moshe and took their leave. Brad could not resist pointing out that Moshe had forgotten his spectacles.

"I can't see properly with those things on," he said cheerfully.

Back at the cottage Brigitte saw the images

immediately. Thrilled with excitement she became frustrated with the blank faces of the men. Greg still could not make sense of it at all.

"Sometimes I wonder what I ever saw in you Greg Little," she exclaimed, casting her eyes upward, "you're so thick."

"But irresistible," he grinned.

"Got it...!" Brad suddenly saw the shadows and lines fall into place. The fainter lines were made by the charcoal, whereas the pencil lines, were had been, firmer and more definite. He had been looking at it the wrong way round. He explained and finally, like a wave breaking, Greg saw it too.

Brigitte breathed a sigh of relief, "Saints preserve us."

"It needs touching up," said Brad, "needs more definition, I wonder if Andre could help."

"If he can see it properly," Greg attempted to redeem his loss of face, "it isn't easy."

Andre proved to be invaluable, seeing the features at once. Much to Greg's surprise he sketched carefully and surely bringing the whole page to life. The features were startling in their clarity.

"Christ its better than a photo-fit," breathed Brad." "A local Estate Agent provided photo copies and they emerged with 10 copies of the men they hated most.

Brigitte insisted that Brad stay with them indefinitely, free to come and go as he pleased, anything he wanted, he had only to ask.

He debated whether or not to inform Dubois. Such pictures of the men would assist in their arrest. He didn't want them arrested, if they were, they would be tried in the courts. Even if found guilty their punishment would be lenient, the evidence was too fragile, a clever lawyer would plead, accidental death. The girl had willingly gone aboard, joined them in drinks, agreed to sex and then panicked, fell and hit her head. They didn't intend to hurt her. They were drunk and frightened and dropped her overboard in panic. They were so, so sorry.' They could even be acquitted. Brad wanted them dead, as dead as she was. No other result would do.

Brad phoned Dubois who was able to give more information. The boat had been identified as the 'Pandora' out of Marseilles. The owners have been interviewed. The records from him had an address that the German Police checked and found to be non-existent, the owner knew no more. The booking in St. Tropez for the mooring was also false. Each payment had been in cash.

"So what now...?" Brad asked angrily.

"Of course we shall continue with our investigation," apologised Dubois. "As always something will turn up and give us more to go on, but we are at a bit of a dead end at present. Be assured we are doing our utmost, m'sieu."

"You'd better be!" Brad snarled. He hung up.

"Greg grinned. "Not one of your favourite people I gather?"

"Pompous little prick! Not fit to investigate a bad smell."

It was then that Brad made his decision. He would go to Don Vittorino. He would find them. The Mafia was big and efficient, merciless! They would help, Vittorino had promised any help he ever needed, and God knows he needed it now. Without it, he would never avenge Michelle or scald the hate from his system.

Don Vittorino welcomed Brad warmly. Following a phone call to the private number Brad arrived for lunch at the Chateau, at Vittorino's invitation. No surprise was shown at Michelle's absence, Don Vittorino was not a person who involved women in business, they should always be available, and decorative, never involved in mans' affairs. He was shrewd enough to see that Brad was deeply disturbed. He was however visibly shaken to learn of the tragic murder, listening carefully as Brad outlined the circumstances, his fingers pressed together, lips pursed, a frown of anger creased his forehead.

"I have come to you Don Vittorino," Brad said quietly, "I don't know what else to do, where to go for help," he hesitated, "I am told you are an important man, well connected, with huge influence."

Don Vittorino's eyes narrowed, growing hard. He

said nothing. Embarrassed, Brad pressed on. "It is none of my business, I do not wish to probe into your affairs it's just that the police mentioned it. I don't wish to know, but I thought perhaps." His voice tailed off, conscious of the tension in Vittorino. To Brads relief he visibly relaxed and smiled.

"It is true I have many contacts, many business interests, and the police can imagine what they like. Rumours of Mafia connections run rampant where wealth is concerned. Many of the stories you may hear are unfounded, the violence and corruption, are more correctly the work of minor gangs of thugs and militants who exist everywhere. However I assume you would like me to locate these people, bring them to Justice."

"The police seem either helpless or disinterested. I can get nowhere." Brad explained the belligerence in the boatyard.

Don Vittorino nodded, "If I can find them, what then Brad? What evidence have you got to support their conviction for murder? How can you be sure the police would succeed in exacting adequate punishment?"

Brad was quiet for a moment. He looked at the elegant man across the table. "I shall kill them all," he said quietly. "I don't care about the consequences, only that I must avenge Michelle. In their case I am their Judge and Jury and I will be their executioner. Nothing else matters."

Don Vittorino looked sympathetically at Brad. He

understood the hatred that was engulfing him, eating away at his insides. Such a fine man, clean in mind and body, hurt and bewildered. His only outlet was violence. For Brad to kill a man was unthinkable. Careful not to inject any derision in his voice, Vittorino asked softly, "have you ever killed a man Brad?"

He shook his head and looked at Vittorino defiantly. "I can kill them with my bare hands if necessary."

His host poured more wine. "Killing is an art," he pushed the glass across the table, "it can be mindless, non-productive, satisfying or an act stimulated by self-preservation, self-indulgence or vengeance. In no case does it leave the person who kills unaffected. The degree of self-destruction varies, depending on the mentality and character of the killer. In your case it could destroy you, leave you unable to tolerate living with yourself even if there were no repercussions. There are adequate laws to punish the guilty. Why not let me find these murderers and perhaps extract a confession. The Police could hardly fail to act upon that."

"No law prevailed when they killed Michelle," he said bitterly, "she was not protected by the humanity of justice. Please help me to do this my way, without her there is nothing now, no future, only the past. If I am to become part of the past, then let it be so."

Don Vittorino looked at Brad thoughtfully for a long moment, and then, on impulse, he finished his wine and rose to his feet. "Come Brad," he said, "come with me..."

He led the way from the terrace into the house. They made their way to the door of the room which had so intrigued Michelle on their first visit. Vittorino pulled a silver chain from his pocket and selected a key, unlocking the door he invited Brad to enter. Brad was astounded whatever he'd imagined the room contained it certainly wasn't this. He gazed across the huge chamber his eyes wide with amazement. Heavily carpeted, the walls lined with mahogany cabinets and racks they contained a vast assortment of guns. Rifles, shotguns, hand guns ranging from ancient duelling pistols to the most modern and deadly. The light reflected off the blue and oiled barrels. The walls were padded. As they walked further, there were swords from the age of the Japanese Samurai, jewelled scabbards, sparkling with reflected brilliance, historical duelling sabres from Germany, the range was immense, a veritable collection worth a fortune.

Don Vittorino smiled at Brad's obvious amazement. "My gun room, guns of every type from historical past to the precarious present, manufactured by craftsmen from the world over in search of violent deaths."

He walked on and flicked a series of light switches. At the end of the long room a tunnel burst into light, a miniature underground railway tunnel thought Brad. The far end covered by a translucent screen, the walls of the tunnel heavily soundproofed. Vittornio touched another switch and the screen glowed. Obviously enjoying the impression the place was having on Brad he unlocked a glass fronted cabinet that held over twenty handguns, each labelled and shining. "Take your pick."

Brad looked at him, puzzled and ran his eyes across the array of guns. Brownings, Lugers, Colts, Smith and Wesson, there was even a Heckler and Koch G36 assault rifle. Vittorino selected a Glock SLP 9 mm pistol, went to a drawer and snapped a loaded clip into the butt. "Try this. I believe the British Police use these, when they need to. The screen," he pointed towards the end of the tunnel, will produce a life sized victim, who will appear unannounced, suddenly. He too is ready to kill. Unless you hit first, lethally, without any hesitation, you become the victim. Assassination," Brad flinched at the word, "is a cold determined act. There is no place for any sentiment, emotion, concern or consideration. No time for thought, to maim or incapacitate. It is fast, accurate, sudden death. No second chance."

Vittorino flicked another switch, two grinning skulls appeared. "If you kill him, the left hand skull glows green, if you are killed, the right hand one glows red. Rather like fun at the fair but with greater implications. This is not a game Brad. I wish to convince you of the odds you face. You are using a gun which is the least emotional instrument of death. If you use a knife or your bare hands the odds are one hundred times greater, ready?" Brad nodded.

Vittorino snapped a switch and the screen came to life empty. Brad gripped the weapon firmly, feet apart arms extended the barrel pointing at the screen.

Suddenly the image of a man appeared, almost a reflection of himself. Brad squeezed the trigger. He missed completely, the skull glowed red, again an image this time to the left of the screen. He fired and a red star appeared on the left shoulder of the image. The skull glowed red.

"You only wounded him," murmured Don.

Three more images and Brad scored one green and then unbelievably the image of a young girl. The skull glowed red. "They kill as well," said Vittorino drily, "you hesitated emotion killed you."

Brad looked totally dejected. Don switched off the lights and took the pistol tossing it into a beize lined box ready for cleaning. "Come," he put his arms across Brads' shoulders, "We both need a drink."

Brad grinned self-consciously, "I didn't do very well did I?"

"At least you lived to say so."

As Brad lifted his glass of scotch he was surprised to see his hands were trembling. The lifelike reproduction from the gun room had shown him how easy it was to boast of murdering, how difficult it really was. His spirits sank. If the police can't find them, and I can't either find or kill them, then the whole thing was a waste of time. His self-deprecation and inadequacy fuelled the hatred even more. Don Vittorino watched the reactions passing through Brads mind. He had felt the same when his own wife was gunned down by rival factions years ago, as a warning for him to mind his own business and not to attempt to extend his then modest, operations. He had paid then, paid a fortune to have the killers slaughtered. The self-satisfaction had worn off, never compensating for Maria's death, never satisfying the emptiness. But... he must help this man who had helped Paul. The code of the Mafia debts must be paid. It was ironic that the man who saved his son now demanded the services of the 'Angel of death.'

"I will help you," as he poured more whisky Brad looked up hopefully. "If you agree, I will arrange for them to be located and executed, but, there are conditions. You must never refer to this conversation. You must forget it ever took place. Neither of us must ever admit to being involved. There is a man who will carry out instructions to the letter. These men will be made aware of the reason they are being dispatched. You must be satisfied with that." He looked hard at Brad. "Think hard before you agree Brad, it is a decision which will affect the rest of your life." He rose and walked across to the door. "I will be back in ten minutes."

Brad sat morosely, hands hanging between his legs, his thoughts chaotic. He now had the chance to wipe these bastards off the earth, if he did not take this chance, another would never present itself. If the police found them and the courts convicted, which was remote, there was no motive, just a senseless sex motivated death. The morons could go free while Michelle lay cold in her grave. Why should they live after destroying two lives? The bitter bile flowed through him. He would accept Don Vittorino's offer.

He listened to Brads' decision. He understood, sad that the violence which had been so much of his life had planted its seed again. With a sigh he accepted the situation.

"I need every detail," he picked up a notebook and pen, "from the start, leave nothing out, and then everything to me. Brad related everything he knew and suspected, forgetting nothing. He passed three copies of the sketch and explained how they had obtained them. Vittorino was impressed. "Very commendable," he smiled, "you have many talents."

Brad returned to Greg's home. He was not to question anything he heard. Vittorino would let him know when matters were settled. Until then, socially he was a welcome guest, whenever he wished.

PART THREE
Chapter 12

Two mornings later an advertisement appeared in the Petit Annonces column of the La Monde paper. Avoir besoin d'emballeur, d'urgence, Packer needed urgently, followed by a telephone number.

Packer glanced through the columns of the La Monde as he did every morning. The paper was delivered to his room in the luxury Hotel Majestique, in Paris, which overlooked the Seine, the muted sounds of the river penetrating and soothing. He was munching on a croissant, his eyes narrowing as he saw the insertion. The telephone number was a blind, merely a code to authenticate the entry. He sighed and finished his coffee. He could only be reached through the columns of the paper, never in one place longer than two days... He protected his anonymity with great care. There were too many people who would like to know who, and where he was. Packer was an assassin a cold professional killing machine, his services sought by the Mafia across Europe. He was the unlikely issue from the union of a New York whore and a wealthy Sicilian greengrocer. He had first killed a man at the age of 16 burying a meat hook deep in the skull of a security guard who disturbed him robbing a dockyard warehouse. His Father shocked and disgusted, had smuggled him to relatives in Sicily where he spent the next four years working in the mountains near Messina. He grew strong and tall inevitably becoming involved with the violence of organized crime. Since then his merciless, dedication and cold animal cunning, ensured that he avoided the law and soon established him as a reliable, though expensive, hit man, for the Mafia, and anyone else prepared to pay. He never used his real name, known only as Packer, a parody on his employment at the time of his first murder. It gave him a warped sense of amusement.

Without haste he showered and dressed carefully. He made his way to the foyer of the hotel and found a public phone. Hotel switchboards were staffed by the nosiest women on the planet, intent on minding everyone's business but their own. He dialled a number and waited. Don Vittorino answered.

"You require some goods packed and dispatched?"

"Oui..."

"Vingt heures, aout huitieme..."

"Bon d'accord," both hung up.

The place was always the same, the huge circular gardens facing the Casino in Monte Carlo. The time was left to Packer depending on his whereabouts. Packer looked at his watch, calculating distance, driving time. Tomorrow night, 8 pm. He returned to his room and lit a Gauloise, feeling no emotion. Later he went shopping. He lazed by the river enjoying the August sunshine and watching the women flaunting their charms and lovers, kissing and cuddling in full view, ignored by the passing crowds of tourists and locals.

Later he ate in a small restaurant which he knew served typical basic food. He drank two beers and left. He drove slowly through the red light district eyeing the women offering their services. He pulled up alongside a group of three girls and beckoned to the prettiest... she looked about 17 years old. She ran over to the car, "Bon jour... do you need some company?"

"Five hundred all night..."

She hesitated, five hundred euros was twice what she usually charged he looked ok. Big man, probably give her a good time as well. She nodded.

"Get in," Packer opened the door and the girl slid in, her dress riding up as she did so.

"My name is Suzanne, what's yours?"

"None of your business just shut up."

Suzanne pouted, "only trying to be friendly," she complained.

"Well don't..." He drove back to the hotel. They got out and Packer walked her through the foyer. The receptionist took no notice, none of his business he thought.

In the room Packer poured two whiskies. Suzanne giggled. "I don't really drink," she said.

"Time you started."

"Shall I take my clothes off?" She wriggled her bottom provocatively.

"No, I'll do that when I'm ready."

He disappeared into the bathroom. He re-appeared wearing a towelling robe. He sat on the bed and looked at her. Not bad, let's see what she's got. He undid her dress and let it slide to the floor, he unclipped her brassiere.

"Careful with my stockings, they're new," she smiled. He turned her round and pulled her panties down. She stepped out of them. He left her stockings alone.

"Right, into bed with you...!"

Suzanne pouted, "you don't take much time do you, I'm here all night. Don't you want me to do anything first?"

The night was an experience for Suzanne. He came over her almost immediately and took her forcibly, thrusting into her almost desperate in his need. When he finished he rolled off her and turned away. Bloody hell, what was all that about? She thought, struggling to get her breath back. Had he finished with her? She had better stay. She turned over and lay still. She was almost dropping off to sleep when Packer turned and pulled her to him. This time he took longer and she began to enjoy him. He certainly knew what he was doing albeit he was a bit rough. The third time he took his time and got out of bed as he finished.

"You certainly want your money's worth," she complained.

"You can fuck off now," he called from the bathroom.

"What? It's still the middle of the night. Let me stay till morning."

"I said Fuck Off! He walked into the bedroom, gathered up her clothes and slung them on the bed.

"What about my money?" Suzanne was bewildered and upset. She hadn't done anything he didn't like, why had he turned nasty.

Packer pulled his wallet from his jacket and peeled off ten, fifty euro notes, and threw them on the bed as well. He hesitated and pulled another fifty out. "Now go... and thank you, that will pay for a cab."

Pacified she dressed quickly. "Will I see you again," she asked timidly.

Packer laughed. "Go on home," he said. Suzanne left.

Packer booked out of the hotel where he had registered under a fictitious name, pleased that the practice of holding passports and identity papers at reception had almost disappeared since the EEC. It had been no problem before, Packer had many passports and false identity papers in a variety of names. But, it had been a nuisance. The Porsche ate the autoroute and spat the kilometres behind it contemptuously. He drove fast, precise, within the speed limits, not stopping until Lyons fell behind him. He drank a beer and demolished a sandwich at a large and immaculate Service Station. Aix en Provence appeared briefly and the ring road skirted the city limits and swung towards Nice. Monaco was reached in good time, the principality glittering in the evening sunshine. Packer chose the third cornice, a high road entering Monte Carlo from the mountains. The Pink Palace, glowing above the city beamed benevolently across the harbour and the Marina, neat and tranquil, with moored boats and yachts of every size and nationality. The roads were quiet. Monaco lived by night.

Winding into the heart of the town Packer slowed, the engine burbling, further on the Casino appeared on his right, flood lit, imposing a magnificent structure portraying sculpted turn of the century themes. He drove slowly into a clear parking spot facing the immaculate gardens. There were no parking meters. Clients of the Casino did not expect to pay for the privilege of risking fortunes on the tables. The clock above the three huge entrance doors showed 7.45 pm. He climbed stiffly out of the car, tucking the newspaper beneath his arm and stretched. His eyes flicked across the illuminated gardens. The usual seat was unoccupied. He walked across, slowly and sat down, opening the paper, not reading, watching. The seat was well away from the iron railings, out of earshot of passers-by. Packer relaxed, enjoying the perfumed air. At precisely 8pm. a typical tourist, dressed in colourful shorts and shirt, with the inevitable camera slung around his neck, ambled in to view. He stopped and took a photo of the

Casino, his flash one of many in the gardens. He stood for a moment or two admiring the flowers. He then made his way to the bench and sat down at the far end, gazing around contentedly. He placed a folded newspaper by his side.

"Under the guise of photographing the landscape," he muttered, "no better place to be."

"Especially in moonlight..." Packer replied.

The tourist fiddled with his camera, picked up Packer's newspaper and ambled off disappearing into the crowd. Packer stayed for a few minutes until a young couple sat on the bench. He then picked up the paper and walked away. He felt the edges of a folder within the paper. He drove along the coast road to Menton and booked into the Hippocampe Hotel. He had stayed there before, the food was excellent, and he needed a drink. Later, well fed and with a large whisky in his hand, he settled comfortably on the bed and opened the folder. He read carefully, his sharp mind absorbing detail, weighing facts. He gazed at the sketch of the three men, imprinting their features deep in his memory. He allowed for variation, moustaches grown, or shaved off. He took a pencil and drew three faint lines down each face. The scars need not still be there, on whom, he didn't know which one Michelle had attacked. The only firm lead was the boatyard in Marseilles. Sliding the folder beneath his pillow he undressed and slid into bed. In moments he was in a dreamless sleep. Three bundles of five hundred thousand euros, nestling in a Swiss Bank account was a superb sedative.

Yvonne was filing her nails, her bottom perched on the desk, legs swinging her thoughts on the next weekends disco, when the office door opened. She looked at Packer suspiciously. Falaise had cautioned her to say nothing to people she didn't know, since the visit by Brad.

"Yes?" She looked at Packer impudently, making no attempt to move.

"Where's Falaise?" He looked at her, cold and arrogant.

"Who wants him?" Yvonne didn't like people who ignored her brash charms. Packer looked at her, his eyes expressionless. Yvonne felt uneasy, sorry she had been so brusque. He's a nasty bastard, she thought, deciding to put the desk between them. "Eyes like a bloody snake. Before she could move Packer bent and grabbed her ankle, jerking it upward and tipping her backwards off the table where she sprawled in a tangle of limbs on the floor. She shrieked, her legs kicking, her short skirt around her waist... Packer looked at her, enjoying the view.

"You touch that phone, you make a sound and I shall slit your throat from ear to ear. Do you understand?"

Yvonne, slumped into the chair and promptly wet herself, she was terrified. Packer walked over and opened the door to the inner office. He slammed the door behind him.

"Who the hell are you?" Falaise snarled, an unlit cigar drooping from his lips. Packer took two steps across the room and jabbed two fingers into Falaise's flabby throat. He fell back into his chair gasping in pain and the shock of the attack.

Packer walked across and gazed out of the window across the boatyard. "Where's Kleiber?" His voice was quiet and brittle.

"Who...?" He swallowed, throat hurting. Christ this bastard was dangerous, not like the other one, it wouldn't be easy to get rid of him. "If you don't get out at once I shall call the police."

"Won't be easy after I slit your fucking throat," Falaise felt sick.

"Kleiber... Hans bloody Kleiber. Where is he?" He picked a delicate glass swan in full flight, from the desk, tossed it in his hand turning it. The sun glinted spreading the colours in glowing beauty.

Anxiously Falaise watched. "Please, be careful that is very valuable, very rare. His heart beat faster as Packer tossed it from hand to hand. "I don't know where he is."

Falaise decided it was no good denying Kleiber completely best to convince the man he didn't know any more. His eyes watched the handling of the glass swan, mesmerised with anxiety. Packer shook his head in mock despair he dropped the swan to the floor. Falaises heart nearly stopped. The glass did not break on the heavy carpet. Packer put his foot on it. The slender neck snapped, with more pressure the fine glass shattered into fragments, He ground them into the carpet. Packer turned towards the table and looked at the remaining glass treasures. Falaise could have wept with hurt and frustration.

"Stop...wait," he pleaded, "I'll tell you all I know, which isn't much." His eyes lingered on the smashed glass with despair. No-one acted like this for Christ sake only the Mafia. That's who he is, the Mafia! His stomach lurched. Why them? Why are they involved? He should have told the other guy more perhaps he wouldn't have this cretin on his back. He could have handled the other one. Packer walked back to the desk, looking at the deflated Falaise as he pulled a ledger towards him and thumbed through the pages. His fingers shook as he turned them. He found the entry.

"Hans Kleiber, 84, Rue de la Madelaine, Nimes Sales Manager for Volkswagen." Falaise looked up helplessly. "He chartered the boat for two, that's all I know, paid cash in advance. I've only seen him twice. I don't know him, that's the truth."

Packer asked for the telephone number of the Volkswagen Head Office and scribbled the number on the corner of the blotting pad sitting on the desk. He ripped the corner off the pad. Falaise said nothing, biting his lip. Packer dialled again, a bright girl answered. Falaise was shaken by the sudden change in his voice. It became friendly, warm and enthusiastic.

"Sorry to worry you, I wonder if you could help. I am looking for Mr. Hans Kleiber, one of your Sales managers, he's been recommended. I'd like to discuss some fairly complicated purchases. Could you tell me where I might contact him?" He waited, "that is most kind, thank you. No I will contact him myself." He hung up and pulled the rolled up sketch from his inside pocket. He unrolled it and held it in front of Falaise. "Which one is Kleiber?"

Falaise nearly fell off his chair in shock. His face went white as his own sons face peered at him, clear and lifelike as a photograph. The others were as accurate. Where in the name of God did this come from? If this bastard was after Kleiber, Pierre wouldn't be far behind. Sweat formed on his forehead, his mouth open, transfixed he pointed to Kleiber.

"The others...?" Packer noticed the panic.

Falaise struggled to control his fear. He didn't know the others, not yet. Pierre was safe for the moment, but if he got to Kleiber...

"I don't know the others, never seen them before, only dealt with Kleiber, really, I would tell you..."

Packer re-rolled the drawing and slid it beneath his jacket, his eyes boring into the frightened man.

"If Kleiber, or the others, or anyone else are told anything, phoned, or contacted I shall return and slit your flabby throat." he said the words chilling, the implications too frightening to ignore.

He left, grinning at Yvonne who cowered back, her eyes wide and scared.

"Pretty knickers..." He smiled. He left slamming the outer door.

As he left Falaise slumped in his chair mopping his forehead, his mind was in turmoil. 'Damn them all to hell, Kleiber, the ugly one and Pierre as well.' His fear turned to anger. Hitching his drooping trousers he stalked out of the office and yelled at Yvonne. "Where's Pierre, get hold of him, get him up here right away."

Yvonne, still shaken rubbed her backside, "He hurt me, bruised my bottom." She complained, "big bully, who is he. Shall I call the Police?"

"Don't you fucking dare...! Mafia that's who he is, the Mafia for Christs' sake. You're lucky he didn't break your stupid neck, now stop rubbing your arse and get Pierre up her."

She scuttled out of the office she'd never seen her boss like this she searched the yard for Pierre. Falaise was picking the broken glass out of the carpet when Pierre entered, puzzled by Yvonne's panic. He had seen Packer leave and kept out of sight, as he had been told to do since Brads' visit. He was startled to see the anger and fear on his fathers' face. Falaise looked up from the broken ornament.

"You've got to get away, far away," hide yourself until this bloody business dies down. Get moving."

Pierre gasped. "Why what's wrong...?"

"Wrong, you're wrong. What you did was wrong. Now the Mafia's after you, Kleiber and the other one, what's his name?"

"Karl," Pierre was trembling.

"They've got a picture of you. All of you, a life like drawing it won't take that bastard long to get your name out of Kleiber."

"He doesn't know where Kleiber is."

"I fucking told him, didn't I?" Snarled his father, "had to or he'd have smashed all these." he waved at the desk and the glass models. "Look at my swan, the swine trod on it."

"I must warn Hans," Pierres face was white, he felt ill.

"Don't you dare…!" Screamed Falaise, "sod Hans, look after yourself, get out and hide, or he'll kill the lot of us."

"Where can I go, I don't know anyone who would have me. I've got no money, no car no friends. I had nothing to do with it, I never touched the girl."

Falaise looked at him sadly, silly bloody kid, always did get into other peoples troubles. He opened an ancient grey iron safe and took out a bundle of 500 euro notes and counted off a wad. He passed them to Pierre.

"Take that, take the car and go to Toulon, it's a big place, he won't find you there if you keep your head down, find some lodgings, just for a while. Now go," he went on gruffly, "in case the fornicator comes back and don't say anything to her," he jerked his thumb towards the outer office, "you know what a bloody blabbermouth she is."

Pierre left, his mind in a whirl he quickly packed a case and drove his fathers' old Peugeot out of the yard. From the office window Falaise watched him leave.

Chapter 13

Packer shifted, uncomfortable on the slatted metal chair. He was outside a bistro on the outskirts of Nimes, a small township named St. Cannat. He glanced at his watch, he had waited for two hours consuming numerous coffees, served by an indifferent waiter, lethargic in the heat. The pavement was emptying slowly, customers returning to work after the long lunchtime break and the township slowly reviving for the afternoon trade. St. Cannat gathered a sizeable trade from passing customers who preferred the Route Nationale N7 to the busy Autoroute, which snaked from Aix en Provence to Valence, Lyon and Paris. Opposite was a large Volkswagen Dealers, the main distribution point for the region. 15 km. from the main city of Nimes, the overheads were less, accessibility easier than in the busy choked town. It was at this dealership that Hans Kleiber was based.

Packer rose and stepped across to the parking meter he thrust two euros into the slot and the needle whirred and sprang across to 60 minutes. It was the second time he had fed the meter, he didn't want any problems. Stretching his lean and muscular frame he ran his hands through his black curly hair, his eyes constantly returning to the showroom opposite. The sun was hot, he cursed the black leather jacket, but he needed it to cover the 357 Magnum holstered under his left arm. He pressed his arm against the comforting hardness of the gun. The main door of the showroom opened, a tall fair man neat in a business suit stepped out carrying a briefcase, hair long to the shoulders. He fumbled in his trouser pocket for keys and unlocked the door of the Sirocco, parked outside. The sun caught his face. Packer could see the three glazed scars, running from cheekbone to chin, white against the tanned face. The Sirocco pulled away toward Aix en Provence slipping into the stream of traffic. Packer threw 10 euros on the table and slid behind the wheel of his Porsche. He was facing the wrong way. Judging the moment he slithered into a u turn greeted by angry horn blasts and flashing headlights and edged into the line of traffic, three vehicles behind Kleiber. He followed, keeping well out of visual distance. After ten minutes Kleiber pulled into the car park of the Carrefour Supermarket, and went in. Ten minutes later he emerged carrying a plastic bag. The car drove away towards Nimes. They skirted the main town and threaded their way into a high class residential area. Expensive properties, set back from a tree lined avenue. The nameplate, attached to a low wall caught his eye. 'Rue de la Madelaine. This was it, Kleiber was home. Packer slowed and watched. The Sirocco slowed down and turned into the driveway of a detached house. He parked and let himself in.

Packer drove past, parked well up the avenue, and retraced his steps. There was a small park almost opposite Kleiber's house. Some children were playing, supervised by their mothers. Packer sat on a seat where he could see the house through the trees. He pulled out a newspaper lit a cigarette and waited. It was 6.15 pm. After half an hour nothing had happened, he was about to return to the car when a white Golf turned into the drive and parked alongside the Sirocco. A woman got out rummaged about in the back and let herself into the house. Satisfied Packer returned to his car and drove into Nimes. There he booked into a hotel, dumped his bag in the room and went into the dining room. After his meal he bought a bottle of whisky from the bar and went to his room. He stripped off, showered and poured a large whisky. Ten minutes later he was in bed and asleep.

The next morning he was back in the park. It was early, no-one else about. He waited. At 8.30 Kleiber emerged and climbed into his car. He drove away. Packer still waited. At 9am the door opened and the woman left, driving in the opposite direction. Satisfied Packer walked to his car and drove back to the hotel. There he packed the items he had bought in Marseilles in a canvas bag, and spent the afternoon ambling around Nimes. The next afternoon he dressed in a nylon set of overalls with electricite de France, printed on the back, he drove to Kleibers house and parked in the next street. Carrying his bag he walked back and rang the doorbell. There was no reply, checking there was no-one around he made his way to the rear of the house, smashing a pane of glass in the back door, he unlocked it and stepped into the kitchen. Kleiber returned home just before 6 pm. He walked into the lounge and stripped off his jacket before he saw Packer sitting motionless in an easy chair.

"Who the bloody hell are you? How dare you break into my home, get out or I'll call the Police." He stuttered.

Packer was out of his chair like a panther and pistol whipped Kleiber. He collapsed, blood pouring from a head wound, lips ripped and teeth splintered mouth gushing blood. Packer dragged him into the centre of the room and hauled him on to an upright dining chair. Rummaging in his bag he found a roll of duct tape and swiftly strapped Kleibers arms and legs to the framework. He added two turns around the body. He sat down and waited for Kleiber to come round he lit a cigarette. Kleiber surfaced through a sea of agony, his head pounding, mouth filling with blood, gagging him. He spat out a broken tooth and struggled to focus on the monster in the easy chair. Packer watched him, enjoying the pain he had inflicted.

"You bastard," he tried to lift his head but sank back with a moan. "What do you want?" His mutilated lips were not able to form the words beyond a mumble.

Packer ambled into the kitchen and returned with a full water jug. He tipped the water over Kleibers head. Kleiber gasped, who was this maniac, couldn't be a thief, a thief would have been long gone. He took a deep breath and thought better than screaming for help, it would only lead to another smashing blow. Packer smiled his eyes cold.

"That's from the girl, you remember the girl?"

Panic flooded through him, the girl, the girl on the boat, my God that was what this was all about. He had managed to push the killing to the back of his mind, enough to convince himself her death could not be connected to him or the others. The sudden realization that this man knew sent a chill of fear through him. How could he know, how did this creature find him. He couldn't think straight, his brain hurt too much.

Packer unrolled the sketch in front of him. "You either die now or you tell me who the other two are and where they are."

Kleiber peered at the portrait through hazed eyes, he blinked, it was impossible, he had destroyed the drawing himself, ripped it into small pieces and flung it overboard, realizing it could incriminate them all. But it was here, in front of him, clear and damning. The need for self-preservation steadied him. He spat out more blood, trying to raise himself against the restraints. If he could get to his feet, get to the door. Packer sensed the desperation in him and raised the Magnum, the cold blue eye of the gun looked unblinkingly into Hans' face.

"Who, and where, or I pull the trigger."

He meant it, Kleiber could see that, there was no escape this man was a killer, if I tell him he'll leave me alone. In order to bide time his wife would be in soon. "Who are you, police?"

"Not police they dont use such brutal methods."

"Call me vengeance, and don't ask questions. I ask you, give me answers." He shook the Sketch.

"If I tell you..." Hans' stopped at the look in Packers eyes.

"I said no questions."

Hans' resistance collapsed, if it meant saving his own life, to hell with Karl and Pierre. Karl had killed her anyway, he hadn't, why should he protect them.

"Karl Brandt, runs a garage and used car firm in Nimes, big place, on the corner, called Paradis Motors... it's on the' Rue Paradis.' It was him, he killed her not me. I didn't touch her."

Packer dragged the gun barrel down the scars on his cheek. "Fucking Liar." he said cheerfully. "Who's the other one?"

"Pierre Falaise," Packers eyes narrowed, he sucked in his breath. He had been on top of that one and didn't know it. "From Marseilles, his father owns the Pegasus Boat Yard?"

Hans was not surprised that Packer knew, he seemed to know everything.

"Now get out."

Packer looked at him, cowardly pig, put up no fight, ratted on his cronies. At that moment there was the sound of a key in the lock and Hans' wife opened the front door. Packer put his finger to his lips and glared at Hans, who thought better than to call out.

The woman walked into the lounge, "Hans, I'm home..." The words died on her lips as she took in the scene. Her husband bound and bleeding, a huge man standing over him. "What the Devil..." Packer shot her dead, a black hole appearing between her eyes. She fell, dead before she hit the floor.

Hans screamed, "You swine...why, why, she's done nothing. Oh my God! He burst into tears and struggled with his pinioned arms and legs.

"You remember I said I would let you live if you answered my questions?" Kleiber couldn't speak, "well I lied." said Packer.

He pulled a long stiletto knife from a sheath at the back of his neck, suspended between his shoulder blades. Calmly he slit Kleibers throat from ear to ear, stepping back as the blood spurted. He waited for a moment as the corpse shuddered and fell still. He then slit Kleibers shirt from neck to waist and sliced open the front of his trousers. He set to work. Later he left through the back door, having picked up the shell case and two cigarette stubs which he dropped in his bag. He stripped off the gloves, which he had worn throughout and put them in the bag. As he left he waved at no-one and walked to his car. There he quickly stripped off the overalls and stuffed them in the bag. He lit a Gauloise and drove off. Karl could wait until another day.

Chapter 14

The national newspapers made no mention of the murder, until two days later, Greg spotted the story first. He always devoured the papers at breakfast time anxious to see if there was anything which could be followed up. News relevant to the Cote D'azure would hold the readers for a day or two after the nationals had discarded them. He shouted to Brad.

"Here come and see this Brad, can't be a coincidence, looks like Vittorino's born fruit." Both Brad and Brigitte read the report.

"Police discovered two bodies, which had lain undiscovered for two and a half days, in Rue de la Madeline, Nimes. The man had been brutally murdered and his wife, shot in the head. Neighbours identified them as M'Sieu and Madame Hans Kleiber. M'Sieu Kleiber was a senior Sales Director with a large Volkswagen distributor. His body had been savagely mutilated. Police are anxious to speak with anybody who may have seen anything suspicious during the afternoon of 15th and the 17th in the vicinity. A special murder investigation unit has been set up in Nimes. Telephone number…"

Brad had told them of his arrangement with Don Vittorino, Greg was dubious of the wisdom in such an arrangement. Brigitte had been openly critical.

"You're wrong Brad," she'd said fervently, "you can't let the dogs of war loose like that, you've no idea what might happen. If you get into the clutches of murdering criminals you'll never be free of sadness and danger. It's the wrong way, leave it to Dubois. Let him catch these people otherwise you'll regret it all your life." Now, having read the report, she blew her top. "It can't be a coincidence, this man Kleiber savagely murdered with a week or so of you going to Vittorino. How do you feel now Brad?" She said scathingly," clean, wholesome, satisfied. Proud of what you've done?" Her eyes flashing, hands on her hips. "You might just as well have done it yourself, at least that would have shown courage...this didn't."

"Oh do belt up Brig," muttered Greg, embarrassed, but feeling much the same way. "Brad didn't realize, did you buddy? He's not a bloody criminal, used to this sort of action."

"Well he's learning fast," snapped Brigitte and stalked out.

Dubois phoned Brad on his mobile the next morning. He demanded that Brad meet him at Cannes Gendarmarie. There was no friendliness in his tone, very officious. Brad was worried at Dubois' change of feelings. He was no longer the injured party, able to dictate from strength, he was now involved in the very same set of circumstances as were Kleiber and his cronies. He was an accessory, as guilty as the hand which had killed, being sought by the law instead of being supported by it. Dubois had given no reason for the meeting. Brad arrived 5 minutes late. Dubois greeted him without the usual warmth, cold thought Brad hopeful that it was his own conscience which suggested the change.

He was taken to an interview room. Brad spoke first. "Do you have some more evidence Inspector?"

Dubois didn't answer then. "You will have seen the report of the double murder in Nimes I expect?"

"I did see something, actually Greg spotted it first. It was the name that caught his eye. Kleiber, coincidentally the name of the man you're after. Is it him?"

Dubois reached for a folder and extracted some coloured photographs. He passed them to Brad. They were taken from all angles of the murdered man and his wife. Brad felt sick as he gazed at the pictures. The body, strapped to the chair, face twisted in the agony of death. His face terribly mutilated, eyes staring in horror. The face and body were drenched with blood, the throat sliced open, gaping like a toothless cavity. Another photograph showed the stomach sliced open like a gutted trout, a mass of entrails a huge blotch across the groin.

"Who's this?" gasped Brad in shocked surprise, pleased that his voice didn't betray anything.

"Kleiber, Hans Kleiber, the man who hired the boat Mam'selle Le Jeune died on. The man we didn't find in time." Said Dubois, he passed another photograph. "You see what was in his mouth...?" It was swollen, black, unnatural, no teeth visible, just a swollen bulge. "His genitals had been severed, penis and testicles and stuffed down his throat. The classical trade mark of the mafia normally carried out before death." Brad pushed the photos away.

"How the hell do you make out I know anything about this slaughter." summoning anger as his best defence, the only way to hide the surging emotions which threatened to make his involvement obvious to the carefully watching Inspector. "It can only have been an intruder, a coincidence, a thief or bloody lunatic. Why kill his wife?"

"I do not believe in coincidence, I never have. The wife obviously disturbed the assailant. Certainly not a thief, no thief would hang about to commit such savagery. What brings me to my way of thinking is, first your natural hate of the men who killed Mam'selle La Jeune, your association with Don Vittorino, his connections with the mafia, the inexplicable death of one of the alleged murderers after a short time and the unmistakable hallmark of a mob execution." Dubois sat back in his chair and looked at Brad severely. "I hope you will not attempt to convince me that these are coincidental. You know far more about this than you have told me, I urge you, no I insist, that you tell me everything that has taken place. If you do then it may be possible to apprehend the others before a similar disgusting fate befalls them, and," he said ominously, "makes it possible to consider your involvement."

Brad denied everything, a decision he was to regret later, insisting that his involvement with Vittorino was no more than social, adamant that he only had Dubois word that, Vittorino, was connected to the mafia. If Klieber was the sort of person who murdered defenceless women, he could well be guilty of other crimes. If the Police had found him in time he would still be alive. Dubois was not impressed by Brads' belligerence. He could sense the anxious, insecurity beneath the surface. Perhaps it was the wrong time to pursue the man, the shock of the photos had been genuine, the realisation would take time to sink in. He would think differently in a few hours. He drew the interview to a close, impressing the need to keep no information back, offering him a chance to change his mind. After he left, Dubois picked up the phone and ordered twenty four hour surveillance on Brad until further notice.

Chapter 15

There were others who read the newspaper. Jacques Falaise read it with horror. He was under no misapprehension, as to who was responsible. Sick that he had been the one to give the information of Kleibers location. He imagined a similar fate for Pierre and shuddered. What could he do, he even imagined closing the boatyard and leaving France. What difference would that make they would still find him and Pierre. He ranted through the office searching his terrified mind for a solution. Swearing at everything including, Yvonne. She kept out of his way, convinced the old fool had slipped his trolley.

Suddenly he stopped, mopping his brow. He would plead, beg, anything for his sons' life. Pierre hadn't killed the girl, had nothing to do with it. They would be satisfied if he paid. That was it he would pay for his sons' life and his own. He burst out in a sweat again. Pay who…. he had no idea who the murdering maniac was, where to find him, he'd have gone to ground, disappeared. The next time he saw him it would be too late, too late to plead, too late to pay. Falaise sank into his chair and groaned.

He suddenly sat up. The first man, the upstart he had flung out of the office, He had wanted Kleiber, probably the girls' husband or lover. He would be the one who put out the contract, he'd listen he had to call off the murdering animal, what was his name Carpenter, Cartwright, Carter that was it, he'd left his card somewhere. He searched his desk drawers, his pockets, nothing. He burst into the outer office.

"That number, telephone number Carter left, where is it?" he yelled at Yvonne.

"Number what number, who's Carter? Yvonne was scared of this fat lunatic. "For Christ sake, the cocky sod I slung out, the first one to ask about Kleiber."

"Oh that," Yvonne said sulkily, "I filed it in the cabinet," she nodded at the grey filing cabinet in the corner.

"No wonder I couldn't find it," Jacques pulled open the top drawer.

"Second one down, first section," she said sweetly, she was proud of her filing system, "what's all the panic about?"

Falaise slung the newspaper at her. "That's what, if I can't do anything your arse will be in a sling as well and mine and Pierre."

He found the card and rushed back into his office, slamming the door shut behind him. Karl Brandt also read the news report, a cold sweat of fear bathing his forehead. He sat in the office of Paradis Motors drinking coffee. The Office was large and comfortable, two modern desks, the floor carpeted, comfortable upright chairs along the walls Paradis was a successful business, established after years of work by Brandt and his partner, Christian Renier. Renier was a skilled mechanic and looked after the garage side of the business, being French he had been the mainstay at first but Karl had rapidly shown a flair for buying and selling used cars. He read the report a second time. The affair had never been out of his thoughts, the worry always there. When Michelle's body had been washed up at Cannes he cursed his luck, he had assumed she would never be found or would be so affected by the sea that identification would be impossible. Since then there had been no further mention of her death and he began to believe that the matter had died down. There was nothing to connect him with the murder, except Hans and Pierre. Pierre would say nothing, his father was too frightened. The slaughter of Hans washed away all his self-convincing arguments. Someone had found Pierre and through him located Hans. Karl had no doubt Hans had died without incriminating him. The spectre of the law had filled his mind before, any other possibility had not occurred to him. God knows the law was preferable to the maniac seeking him out. He looked up from the report. He must get out of here, the garage was too easy to find. He was a sitting duck, unprotected, one bullet through the glass, he shuddered. He rose and walked through into the main repair shop. Christian Renier was inspecting the work carried out by a newly employed apprentice, his overalls smeared with grease. He acknowledged Karl with a nod.

"I have to go away for a while," Brandt tried to keep

his agitation from his voice, "something has cropped up at home."

Christian looked surprised, "not bad news I hope."

"No, no, just something I must see to."

Renier shrugged, not like Karl to be cagey, but then, he had been on edge since his holiday. "I can't do it all, who's going to look after the sales side, the garage takes all my time now and business is always heavy as summer starts. Can't it wait? You haven't long had a holiday?"

Karl shook his head, "It can't wait, too urgent, I'll keep in touch." He had said nothing to anyone about the death of the girl. "If anyone asks for me, say you don't know where I am. Dorothea can look after things, as long as you vet anything major."

Renier was even more startled, 'What sort of trouble was he in?'

"As you wish." Christian realized he would get no more from Brandt. He turned back to the waiting car. Dorothea was due to arrive in ten minutes she was a thin and efficient woman who looked after the finances and paper work. Brandt went back to the office he couldn't spare the time to wait for her. He scribbled a note and left it on her desk. He collected some things and left the building.

He looked at the Peugeot 504, the company run-about car and decided against it, turning towards a Mercedes 450 SEL sports car, gleaming in the sunshine.

He had bought it at a bargain price, had it checked, it was in superb condition. He had earmarked it for himself until he found a buyer who would pay a good price. The keys were in it. He drove into the stream of traffic, eyes alert, seeking, watching for anything different. He didn't see the Porsche parked 50 metres away, on the opposite side of the road. Packer watched the Mercedes pull out and drive away. He wasn't sure. The building had hidden the driver as the car stopped. Waiting for a break in the traffic his face had been turned away at a crucial moment. Packer played a hunch and slipped the Porsche into a space behind a large tourist coach. The road widened as a large, lightly controlled junction approached. He eased into the right hand lane and drew alongside the coach. The lights were red, the Mercedes in the centre lane waiting for the green. An arrow turned green for Packers lane, indicating right only. He hadn't realized a horn blared immediately behind him. Packer stayed where he was, cursing, he didn't want any attention called to him. The horn, and others, blared again and Karl looked over his shoulder straight into Packers face, curious about the horn.

It was Brandt, no doubt at all, the features imprinted in Packers mind. Packer smiled to himself, his hunch had paid off. The horn blared again, longer this time, the driver impatient to turn right. He was saved from further embarrassment by the main light turning green. He slipped swiftly in front of the coach only to be blasted by a two tone klaxon from the coach driver. He followed directly behind the open topped Mercedes, annoyed that he should have been exposed so soon to Brandt. Worried people noticed things he had lost a certain amount of control. As soon as there was an opportunity Packer thrust his way past the Mercedes, watching carefully in his mirror. Brandt noticed him go by, no more suspicious than he was of any other car. He felt a thousand eyes boring into him, every car contained a killer. Every time a car slowed he felt a bullet smashing into him. He drove swiftly to his apartment on the western outskirts of Nimes, pulled into the private car park of the estate, inserting a plastic card into the electrically operated barrier. The red and white arm rose and lowered with a judder as he drove through, even that made him feel safer. The estate was laid out with ornamental gardens, parking was for residents only. There was no immediate car park for visitors, outside the barrier it was a long walk to the apartments. Packer had seen the Mercedes turn right, in his rear view mirror. He swore he would have to join the other carriageway to get back. He sped towards an opening and did an illegal u turn into the other lane. He cruised towards the estate, not knowing whether Brandt had entered or passed the complex altogether and continued into the low hills beyond. He pulled in the visitors' car park and waited. Brandt drove around the buildings and left his car outside the entrance, not bothering to park in his reserved space he ran up the stairs and let himself into his apartment. He locked the door firmly, still unaware of the predator waiting.

He relaxed a little, feeling safer inside the flat. He quickly checked the place, switching off the gas and electricity he poured a beer and started packing a small suitcase. He wouldn't need a lot. In the bottom drawer he uncovered a small Colt Cobra pistol, a box of shells by its side. He hesitated, the gun had been found in a used car sold to him months ago, hidden in the folding rear seat arm rest. It had never been claimed. He slid it into his pocket with the bullets, comforted by the weight against his thigh. He poured another beer. With a last look around he picked up the case and left. He walked slowly to his car, eyes carefully checking. He drove towards the barrier slipping the card into the slot. He passed the visitors car park. The Porsche sat, squat and frog-like in the gravelled area. Brandt's memory flickered. The traffic lights, horns blaring that had been a Porsche. He cursed himself for being so worried 'Porsches are ten a penny here.'

He drove away warily and turned on to the main road to the autoroute. He stopped at the Bank, the Societe Generale which lay back from the road. He drew out 10,000 euros. The teller looked surprised at the amount, "business deal," muttered Brandt, "nosey bastard, it's my bloody money."

As he pulled away he saw a Porsche idling by the bank entrance, His heart beat faster. It was impossible to read the number plate in his rear mirror. He drove away and swung into the autoroute intersection, collected a ticket at the Peage control. There was no sign of the Porsche. The Mercedes leapt away towards

Montpelier. The 60 km to Montpelier disappearing swiftly he continually flicked his eyes at the rear view mirror. He saw nothing, the traffic sparse in the long stretches, thickening slightly as the town approached. He by passed Montpellier and pulled into a service station for petrol. While the tank was being filled he went to the toilet area, freshening himself, splashing cold water over his face, the heat was building up. His clothing was unsuitable he wished he had stopped to change from his business suit.

He walked back to the car and stopped in his tracks, two pumps behind him was the Porsche, an attendant holding the pump nozzle deep in the tank. Packer stood nonchalantly by the car door, tall, relaxed, a sardonic twist on his lips as he saw Brandt's sudden shock. So he saw me did he? He must be shit scared. His black eyes bored into Brandt's face intentionally mirroring recognition and transmitting violence. Brandt paid hurriedly, his heart pounding, the same car, same man, he remembered him from the lights, too much of a coincidence. The bastard had caught up with him already.

Stomach churning he drove away, intent on losing the Porsche somehow. He drove the next 100 kms in a state of panic. He saw the dark squat shape twice behind him. Before Narbonne the autoroute curved to the right, cutting out visibility to the rear. He floored the pedal and shot off at 190km.p.h. His heart fluttered as a car hurtled in view, lights flashing imperiously. A Ferrari swept by effortlessly. The end of the autoroute was signposted. He fished in his pocket for money and was through quickly. Perhaps he could lose the damned car on the smaller roads. There was no place to run on the autoroute. He swung into the slip road to Perpignan the N9 was a wide road. He sped away. There was no sign of the Porsche. He climbed across the Albres Mountains and pulled up at the La Junquera frontier post. The traffic was heavy, holiday makers entering Spain, cars filled with excited children, irritated women and impatient drivers. He sat, waiting, continually looking back willing the queue to thicken. He passed through Spanish Customs and made for Gerona on the national route. It was there that he saw the Porsche again, three cars behind. Deciding to make certain he pulled up in a small service road. The place was crowded, he was safe here. He watched the Porsche. Packer pulled up, leaned out of the window and fixed Brandt with the same threatening look, leaving no doubt in Brandt's mind.

'Right you swine,' he thought, summoning new courage from somewhere, 'you're not going to find me like you did Hans.' He slammed the car into gear and sped off, swinging left on to a small c road to Llagostera' and 'San Felui. He knew the Costa Brava well. At this time of year he could lose the bloody murderer until he could make it to Barcelona. He had friends there. They'd help. Brandt drove fast, as fast as the narrow road allowed. He was exhausted, mentally and physically. The road narrowed even more, the surface worn and damaged by the heat of the sun softening the tarmac.

As he turned a bend there was a motel set back off the road. He looked in his mirror, no sign. He swung into the car park and drove between two lorries on the far side. He jumped out and hid behind one. The car was out of sight of the road. He waited. Sure enough, less than a minute behind him, the Porsche drove by, slowed and then carried on. He still waited and could hear the growl of the engine fade away into the distance. He still crouched behind the lorry. Cautiously he made his way to the reception.

A tired man dozed behind the desk. He looked up. "A room for the night please," he said.

The man yawned and got up, he reached for a key. "Half the nights gone," he grumbled," sliding the register across. Brandt signed a fictitious name. He paid in euros.

Satisfied that the Porsche was well on its way through the Gararras Sierras Mountains, Brandt walked along the dimly lit pathway and let himself into the room. A last check through the window, he pulled the curtains and stripped off to his underwear. He collapsed on to the bed, his mental worries overtaken by the need for sleep. Within minutes he was in a deep sleep with the gun under his pillow. Packer had spotted him. As he drove past he saw the glow of the brake lights as the rear end of the Mercedes slid between the juggernauts. But he drove on accelerating as he went so that Brandt booked into the motel! That was no place for what Packer had in mind. Too many people who could see him or be disturbed, time for Plan B.

One km further on he passed a lay by which offered a parking area to enable sightseers to gaze across the countryside as it swept upward into the Sierras. He reversed and turned in, parking at the far end facing the way he had come. Locking the car he walked back to the motel. All was silent and lit only by the dim light from the reception. There was no sign of life. Quietly he moved around the outer edge towards the juggernauts. It was there, the same Mercedes, he needed to be sure. He returned to his car. He closed his eyes and slept for an hour. The road was silent. On waking, rummaging about in the boot he unlocked a compartment in the floor and pulled out a small package wrapped in chamois leather. Inside was a square of what looked like cheese. There was a mobile phone wired into it. Carefully he placed it on the seat and plugged in the charger. An hour later he looked at his watch, it was 3 am. Outside the night was pitch black. He unplugged the charger and stowed the package in his bag, put on a pair of disposable overalls and a plastic gloves. He set off back to the motel. All was still silent. As he reached the Mercedes he slid underneath, the exhaust was still warm. Swiftly he attached the package to the frame below the driver seat and pressed a button, activating the phone. Silently he returned to the Porsche.

Chapter 16

Manuel Robres slammed the pick into the hardened red earth and cursed for the hundredth time. He straightened his aching frame and swept the battered sombrero from his balding head, mopping his forehead with a grimy, sweat soaked piece of cloth. Even his long drooping moustache was wet with sweat. Even at this early hour it was 30 degrees. He called down the wrath of the Church on all he could think of, Governments, tourists, tax collectors, and mostly ungrateful brothers. He crossed himself fervently, conscious of his blasphemy against his brother. His brother was a pig, a worthless greedy lazy pig lured into the big cities by the promise of a fortune extracted from the tourists. No wonder he had been knocked down and killed by a bus. Like Manuel he was not used to buses.' He belonged to the land, as he, Manuel, belonged. He should have stayed where he was instead of getting above himself. Manuel picked up another rock and slung it deftly into the cart. The ancient mule didn't move, stood braced against the increasing weight of the battered cart, past caring about anything. He was old, his joints and body ached, his eyes, rheumy and sad, protected against the piercing sun by a straw hat tilted over his head, secured by his ears poking through ragged holes. The cart was standing on the land, back end pointing in the direction of the narrow coast road with the blue azure sea pounding on the rocks 300 feet below it. A large rock was wedged behind the wheel but that didn't take the full weight of the heavy granite debris Manuel was clearing. The land had been his brothers, untended for years, allowed to grow into barren rock strewn earth. Manuel gazed longingly at the sea, he loved the sea, his father had been a fisherman, living by, and from the sea. There had been money in those days. Now there was no money, the fish were gone, the pollution and over fishing had seen to that Dios Santo protect us from all tourists.' He slammed into the earth again loosening another chunk of rock. He had to clear the land the Government had threatened to take possession if it remained barren. Manuel took a drink from a flask of tepid water. He cupped some in his hands and held it to the mule, it lapped gratefully.

"They'll build more villas, make more money. Very little would come to him though."

A creak of protest from the timber cart made Manuel look up. He had been so engrossed in his thoughts he hadn't noticed how the cart had been filling up. There was enough in the cart, too much. He frowned and threw the pick down. Taking the worn leather halter he coaxed the mule, cursing his stupidity in positioning the cart as he had. The mule strained, his joints creaking, shoulders hurting. The strain was too much, its heart, pumping with the exertion, flickered and fibrillated and stopped. With what sounded like a sigh of relief, the animal sank to the ground, the weight of its body twisting the cart and snapping one of the shafts. The movement shifted, the restraining rock and the cart took charge, moving slowly at first but gathering momentum dragging the dead mule in its wake. It bounced and slithered towards the flimsy fencing separating the land from the narrow road 20 feet below. Manuel stood shocked. Helpless he watched as the cart tipped over the edge flipping the mule's carcass into the air and taking it with it, plunging out of sight, ripping away the fencing as it went.

The next morning Brandt awoke the anxieties still in his mind. He showered and dressed in clean clothes and stuffed his suit into his case. He was very hungry but didn't trust the motel to provide anything remotely edible. He opened the door cautiously and looked out. The juggernauts were still there. Quickly he walked across and climbed into his car. He backed out slowly and drove to the edge of the road, still no sign of anything untoward. Turning towards San Felui he drove away. As he began to feel confident he passed the lay by. The bloody Porsche was there, squat and threatening.' Jesus Christ this bastard was uncanny,' what was his game. There had been opportunities to shoot him or force him off the road. This was cat and mouse.

What did he want? T that was it, information about Pierre so he could kill him. Brandt drove fast, too fast for the road conditions but he was panic stricken. This time the Porsche stayed on his tail. As the cart and the dead mule disappeared over the edge of his land, Manuel was transfixed with horror. Sweeping his sombrero from his head he crossed himself, fervently.

Gathering himself he ran to the edge and peered over. The road was blocked, completely blocked with rocks and debris strewn across the narrow road. Helpless, he stared, tears filling his eyes with sorrow for his lifelong friend, the gallant little animal who worked so hard and so willingly. His thoughts were disturbed by the sound of an engine. The snarling growl assaulted his ears. He was used to the sound of vehicles passing below, adjusted to the sound of cautiously driven cars. He had never heard an engine make this noise. The racing power was a harbinger of doom. He stood, aghast as the Mercedes swept into view around the tight bend. The Mercedes slammed into the pile of rocks, the front end rearing up like a startled horse and turning in mid-air toward the chasm of the cliff below. It smashed on to the edge of the road and hovered precariously, overhanging the 300 feet drop.

Packer stopped in time. He stepped from his car and could see Brandt struggling to release his seat belt. Grinning, Packer stood, enjoying the sight of Brandt struggling to release himself, hampered by the airbag which had forced him back. He pressed the send button on his mobile. The car erupted in an explosion which even surprised Packer, the vehicle disintegrated into a mass of twisted metal, the flames shot high into the air, the heat felt by Packer metres away. The mangled wreck tumbled into the void somersaulting down the cliff face. Again it exploded as the petrol tank blew up scattering the remnants of the car and Brandt

Packer pulled a warning triangle from the boot and

placed it 50 metres behind his car, he didn't want something smashing into him. He returned to the scene. It would be hours before the road was clear. He got in and carried out a three point, drove back past the motel and over the border back into France. The last thing he wanted was to be questioned as a witness. Some 25 kms later he booked into a hotel, stripped off his overalls and showered. Ate well and again took a bottle of whisky to his room. He slept soundly through the day.

Part Four
Chapter 17

Brad became totally depressed following the interview with Dubois. He couldn't get the horror of the photographs out of his mind. The brutality of the attack sickened him. Brigitte had become distant, her disapproval, although not voiced, was obvious by her attitude. Greg did his best to ease the atmosphere to little avail. Brad continued to brood, not regretting the death of Kleiber, his hatred still smouldered, but to feel he was responsible for the unleashing of such sadism shocked him. It was therefore a great relief to Brigitte and Greg, when Brad decided to call off the assassin. He would go to Vittorino and put an end to the manhunt, after that he would make a clean breast of things to Dubois and leave everything to him. Brigitte was delighted, secretly hating the aloof manner she had treated Brad with but pleased her ruse had worked. She felt desperately sorry for the man, but he had been wrong, Thank God, he had seen it for himself.

Brad drove to Cannes lighter in heart than he had been for a long time, the burden of guilt weighing less now that he had made the decision. He was not aware of the unmarked police car which followed him. He was ushered through the main gates without problems, Vittorino expecting him, unaware of the reason for the visit, but suspecting a change of heart. Brad felt uncomfortable in the presence of Vittorino. He recalled his insistence that the arrangement should never again be mentioned, their conversation forgotten. He steeled himself and told the impassive man how he felt.

"I didn't know such methods would be employed, I wanted them dead yes, but to be slaughtered and mutilated like that. I feel it is best if the police handle everything, they have more to go on now."

Don Vittorino looked at Brad, his features set, a frown of displeasure creasing his forehead. "You remember I insisted that a conversation such as this, should never take place. The arrangement was to be forgotten, erased completely."

Brad nodded, "I," his reply was silenced as Vittorino raised his hand.

"I warned you at the time that such decisions are not lightly made. To release the sword of Damocles is a very final step. I cannot help you Brad, even if I were willing to do so, I cannot stop matters now. I cannot contact the man I have directed, the machine is in motion things must take their course. I understand how you feel, but, you cannot change horses in midstream. You had ample opportunity to make the decision which you felt was right for you."

Brads' heart sank, he could see that Vittorino was adamant, there could be no change of mind beneath the charming and sophisticated exterior, he was as cold, and aloof as an iceberg.

"I must warn you," he went on, "any disclosure to the authorities would meet with an outright denial by myself and would create a very dangerous situation for you."

The threat was hardly veiled. Brad realized he was dealing with a man who placed self-preservation above all things in life. If he told Dubois everything now, nothing would be gained and he could easily become a victim of Vittorinos assassin. Brad left, Vittorino becoming the charming host as they walked to the car, talking affably about general things as though they were at a Garden Fete. Brad drove away even more depressed, not knowing what to do.

Dubois was informed about Brads visit. He decided to pay another visit to Falaise, he was sure that man knew more than he said.

Jacques Falaise was not at all pleased when Inspector Dubois entered the office. Surely to God he had been through enough of this business. "How can I help this time?" He asked wearily.

"Just a few questions M'sieu, they can, perhaps, save a man's life. I need to know the name and address of the other men involved in the investigation. One has been brutally murdered and the same fate could easily befall the others, unless you help. Who are they?"

"I have told you time and time again I do not know. Hans Kleiber was the only one I dealt with. I saw the others but I never did know their addresses."

"Can you describe them?"

"No. I see so many people and there was no reason to have any interest in them."

Yvonne was listening to their conversation. "I know," she said.

Dubois turned to her, and Falaise glared panic stricken at her. Yvonne was still smarting from the treatment Packer had dished out. Pig that he was she could get her own back if he was caught.

"I only know the address of one of them, never seen the other. He signed the insurance cover on behalf of all of them."

She went to the filing cabinet and ruffled through the documents. She pulled a sheet out, headed, 'Assurance Co. de France and passed it to Dubois. It was signed K. Brandt. The address was Paradis Motors Nimes.

"Why did you not tell me this before M'selle," Dubois was angry, "it could have made a big difference."

"Never thought of it," sniffed Yvonne. Falaise relaxed he had wondered whether she was about to drop Pierre in the shit.

Satisfied he'd obtained as much information as possible, Dubois left, he drove to Nimes.

Christian Renier wiped his greasy hands and greeted Dubois as he walked into the office. Anticipating business, he was taken aback when Dubois showed his badge.

"Sorry to disturb you M'sieu, I am looking for Karl Brandt, would he be here?"

Renier shook his head, "I don't know where the hell he is Inspector. He left days ago. Suddenly shot off like a rat with its arse on fire. Didn't say where he was going or why, something to do with problems in the family."

"Dubois looked concerned, "does he live on the premises?"

"No, he has an apartment, on an estate about a mile away. Doubt whether he's there though. He was in a bit of a panic when he left. He took the Mercedes so he was going some distance."

"May I have his home address?" Renier wrote it down and gave directions.

He watched Dubois as he left, 'What the hell was going on, he thought, got himself in some sort of trouble, that guy was from the Surete, could be serious.' He shrugged and went back to work. Dubois found the apartment and was surprised to see two Gendarmes prowling around. He introduced himself and asked why they were there.

"We have been asked by the Spanish police Nacional to confirm this address, a fatal accident at La Junquera. Number plate of the car shows a Karl Brandt as the owner. There appears to be no-one here. All locked up, no-one has seen him for weeks."

"Are they sure the driver was Brandt?" Asked Dubois.

"Only that he owned the car, we know nothing more."

Dubois returned to his offices in Cannes and immediately requested full details of the accident from the Spanish Police, including photographs of the scene. As it was the Surete involved were not long in supplying full details and photographs of the devastation. The body, only part of which had been recovered was so badly incinerated that identification, visually, was impossible. It had been taken to the pathology Dept. of the Santa Maria hospital, in Barcelona. He phoned. Doctor Claude Berlian was a leading forensic pathologist, with a fiery reputation and not afraid to vent his displeasure on any unfortunate who upset him. He was, however very thorough, a stickler for detail. Inspector Dubois had heard of him through his lectures given in perfect French, but never met. The receptionist at the hospital put Dubois through, and Berlian answered.

"How can I help Inspector?"

"The fatal accident at La Junquera, has the cause of death been established."

"Cause of death! I have in front of me fragmented pieces of what was a human being. Totally incinerated! Impossible to identify an arm from a leg, yes, I can tell you the cause of death, he was blown to bloody bits. Does that help?"

"Is there any possibility that a DNA sample could be

obtained?"

"We are not a bunch of amateurs Inspector. Of course we took a sample. Routine, hell of a job, we found what was once a right arm with flesh which escaped the blast, shielded by the body."

"Thank you Doctor, no doubt the Pathology report will be forwarded to us together with the DNA."

"Why do you need this for Inspector, it is Spanish business?"

"Murder, Doctor, This is a murder enquiry, related possibly to a previous killing."

"I see, in which case there are a couple of things you should know inspector. According to a witness, a farm worker Manuel something or other, who saw the accident, there were two explosions. One took place almost immediately after the car collided with the landslide. The other when the petrol tank exploded half way down the cliff. In my experience the heat generated by an exploding petrol tank would be nowhere near the intensity to incinerate car and driver. I am faced with charcoal, not a burned body. This was a bomb, either exploded remotely, or by the impact. I favour the first."

Pierre also read the newspaper report of the murder of Hans Kleiber. As he drove away from his fathers' boatyard, scared and worried by his father's desperation, he thought only of putting as much distance as possible between him and Marseilles. His father had always tended to panic over the least thing, always seeing problems where there were none. Perhaps he was over-reacting this time. Mind you the man he had seen leaving the office looked bloody dangerous, but, as an angel of death and destruction? He didn't think so.

His anxiety faded after all he hadn't done anything really. If he had interfered the other two would have slung him overboard. Perhaps, if he went to the police, told them everything? But that would mean involving Karl. It was Karl who had killed her. If he involved him, Karl would be gunning for him as well. He drove on to Toulon. In the city he pulled into a large underground car-park. Locking the car he made his way on to the street and looked around, was he far enough away? He didn't know Toulon very well. He had been to a disco with Yvonne, some time ago. His memory flitted back, that had been a good night, Yvonne flirting with anything in trousers, and her friend, what was her name? Marie Louise, that was it, wide eyed and soft, she had been quite struck on him. He warmed as he remembered. Perhaps she would know of somewhere he could stay. He tried to remember where she lived, a flat somewhere, he had been there, stayed the night. He'd never find it again he thought, they all look the same. The Supermarket, of course she worked there as a checkout girl. Codec, no not Codec, the Euro Marche, that was it, part of the gigantic Hypermarket. Recovering the car he drove towards the Industrial quarter, the huge Grand Var shopping Mall appeared on his right. He drove into the car-park and walked into the air conditioned building. Euro March was the first of the many stores he saw. He passed the barriers of tills, long queues at each one and looked at all the girls. No sign of Marie. He walked up to a male supervisor and asked for her.

"What is her last name?" Pierre had no idea he didn't think he had ever known it. The Supervisor looked at him suspiciously.

"I met her at a disco," he blurted out, embarrassed, "She left her scarf behind. I want to return it."

"We have a girl, Marie Louise Poitier, she is on late lunch," he glanced at his watch, "be back at 3pm but the girls are not allowed to talk to friends," he said frowning.

"I shall only be a minute."

The supervisor nodded and walked away.

It was half past two. Pierre ambled around the aisles aimlessly. As it drew near to 3 pm, he stood, watching the check-outs. Just before three a dark attractive girl, her hair short and shining smilingly took over one of the desks and signed the roll, sliding on to the seat smoothly. It was Marie Louise. She settled herself, adjusting her skirt. 'She looks good in red,' thought Pierre eyeing her full breasts. He remembered her breasts! He queued up wishing he had a full trolley to give him more time to speak with her. Perhaps she wouldn't remember.

Marie Louise did remember. Her eyes lit up as she

saw him, recognition immediate, two small creases appeared at her mouth as she smiled.

"Pierre, how nice, where have you been?"

Pierre was aware of the frowns from impatient shoppers waiting to come through. "Can we talk Marie, a coffee perhaps when you've finished?"

Marie nodded happily, "I finish at five, another two hours I'm afraid, can you come back?" She looked at him hopefully.

Pierre nodded, "I'll wait, see you in the bar over there." He nodded toward a sunken bar surrounded by climbing plants.

"Oui bien sur." She slid groceries across the till. Pierre walked away, pleased, his heart lighter, more hopeful.

Pierre walked across to the Maison de la Presse, and bought two newspapers, and a boating magazine. He settled into a corner chair and ordered a beer. He could just see the head of Marie Louise bobbing. He browsed through the papers, his mind on the girl rather than the news items. It was the name Kleiber that concentrated his mind and brought his attention back to the paper. He read the report twice before the implications sunk in. he felt himself tighten inside. The bastard he had seen was a killer, he had only got out in the nick of time.' Karl, had he found Karl. Pierre anxiously scanned the pages .Nothing. He read the article again. He sat back and lit a cigarette, his fingers were trembling. Mafia, his father had called him, 'The Mafia.'

It wasn't their scene; surely they weren't interested in the death of a girl. Had Kleiber said anything, told them Karl's address told them about Pierre. Did Karl know? His mind spun like a top. He had to know if Karl was ok. Swallowing his beer he walked quickly to the public phones nearby and searched the directory. It was the wrong one, Nimes was in a different region. He dialled 10 the operator answered. "Paradis Motors Nimes please." He remembered the address, Karl was forever boasting about his business. Given the number Pierre dialled. Dorothie answered.

"May I speak with Karl please?"

Dorothie hesitated. "Who is calling?"

"Pierre, Pierre Falaise, I'm a friend of his."

"I'm sorry, M'sieu Brandt is not here."

Dorothie remembered the instructions on the note she had found, not understanding, but loyal to the directions.

"When will he be back?"

"I have no idea. I'm afraid, he's urgent business elsewhere."

"I must get in touch with him, it is urgent. Can you give him a message, or give me his mobile phone number?"

"I can leave a message, yes but I don't know when he

will receive it. His mobile number is private."

"Please tell him Pierre phoned and that I must speak with him urgently. Ask him to leave word where I can ring him, with Yvonne at the office."

"Will he know the number?"

"Yes…" Pierre hung up.

He returned to the bar unhappy and frustrated that he knew so little. He thought about the police again but was too frightened. He might escape a murder charge but would spend the rest of his life in prison. Only Karl could confirm that Pierre had nothing to do with the actual rape and death, but that would mean Karl admitting he had done it. Perhaps they could blame Hans he was dead and couldn't argue now. His thoughts were interrupted by Marie Louise eager to see Pierre again she had quickly changed and carefully rouged her lips. 'Fancy him turning up like this. She liked him. He was quiet and gentle not like the other brutes she had to fight off. She had been disappointed when he hadn't contacted her again. She had assumed he didn't like her! Perhaps she hadn't been good enough at the pillow, she'd done her best. She was just nineteen, thrilled to have left home to fend for herself although she visited her parents once a week, sure of one good meal and coaxing her mother into doing her washing. She chatted away to Pierre, her coffee going cold, wanting to know where he had been, why no calls, telling him with wide eyes how pleased she was to see him. Pierre warmed to her she was just what he needed. There was no-one else. She would believe him, perhaps even help. Slowly he related the circumstances from the beginning, his confidence increasing as he saw the concern in her eyes. Her eyes widened with horror when he showed her the cutting in the paper of the brutal murder of Kleiber.

"I did nothing Marie," he finished lamely, "I didn't touch the girl, I didn't know they had killed her until I went below. Perhaps I should have stopped them but I was too scared." He looked at the shocked girl unhappily. She took his hand and squeezed. "You poor boy," she looked at him fondly, "What will you do, you can't go home until everything is over, it's too dangerous.

"I wondered whether you would know of somewhere I could stay for a while, so I can think, work something out. Perhaps get in touch with Karl."

Pierre looked at her hopefully. "no problem," she grinned, "you must stay with me." She smiled coquettishly. She would look after Pierre. It would be lovely. She hugged his arm as they walked out.

Packer arrived at the private lock up garages. He unlocked one and walked in. He pulled the cover off a top of the range, Audi saloon. It started first time. He drove out and reversed the Porsche into the garage, covered and relocked the garage. 'No sense in taking chances. Someone may have seen him, noted the index number, better safe than sorry.'

He drove to a favoured hotel and went to his room where he showered, pulled on a robe and opened a bottle of beer. There were still things to be done. He settled down and opened the file, one more to take out. No probably more than one the son and his father. Falaise knew him, so did the little tart in the office only fear had kept their mouths shut so far. He ordered from room service. There was time, no rush to plan his next move.

Chapter 18

Brad explained the adamantcy of Don Vittorino to Brigitte and Greg who listened worried and anxious, seeing the situation worsening, the physical danger increasing, the mental strain telling on Brad.

"It makes no difference Brad," said Brigitte, "You must still tell Dubois, tell him everything. If you're honest and lay your cards on the table he'll protect you. If you don't, you'll be hunted like they are."

Brad agreed grudgingly, he wasn't looking forward to meeting Dubois again, but it had to be done, he could see that.

Greg grinned at him, "I'll come, if you like," he said more jovially than he felt, "bit of moral support. I need to know which Prison you'll be in anyway."

Brad looked at him coldly. Brigitte glared. Great oaf she thought, 'he says the nicest things. The phone shrilled and Greg picked it up. He glanced at Brad offering the receiver.

"It's your office," he said covering the mouthpiece, "Are you here?"

Brad nodded and took the phone, he was surprised they hadn't phoned before, must be wondering what the hell was going on. It was Mac, the Editor. He was called Mac because although born and bred in Paris, he had learnt

English from a tutor who must have lived in the Outer Hebrides and spoke with the same broad Scottish accent. He didn't waste time on niceties, knowing a little of the circumstances.

"A worried guy from Marseilles has been phoning almost on the hour sounds desperate, says he must speak with you. I didn't tell him where you are, wants you to phone him back. Life or Death he said, name of Falaise from Marseilles, Do you know him?"

Brad caught his breath, 'Falaise, what could he want. "Thanks Mac, yes I know him." Brad scribbled down the phone number. Mac hung up. Greg and Brigitte were as astonished as Brad. "Wonder what that fat little swine wants?" muttered Brad.

"How did he know where to find you?" asked Brigitte puzzled.

"I left my card," remembered Brad, "just in case he changed his mind, he obviously knew more than he said at the time."

"Obviously got some information probably panicked over Kleiber."

Greg nodded to the phone. "See what he wants, can't hurt." Brad dialled.

Jaques Falaise had been in a sweat of fear, every time the phone rang, or the outer door opened his heart had hammered. He had phoned the number Carter had left time and time again. He could get no information the man wasn't there. Messages hadn't been passed he

160

hadn't phoned back. His phone jangled, Falaise picked it up as though it would bite.

"This is Brad Carter. You've been trying to reach me."

Jacques Falaise felt faint, the breath poured from his lungs in a sigh of relief. "Thank God I have reached you M'sieu Carter." His voice was servile wheedling. Greg picked up the extension and listened also. "We must meet as soon as possible it is important."

"What's this all about Falaise?" Brad's voice was cold, unhelpful and bitter with the recollection of the previous meeting. "You didn't seem too pleased about seeing me before."

"A misunderstanding M'sieu," there was pleading in the voice, "I was not, not myself, you must forgive me. I cannot talk on the telephone, where can we meet I will come wherever you say, whatever time you wish."

Gregg nodded vigorously as he met Brad's eyes. "As soon as possible," Greg murmured, "but not Marseilles."

"Very well Falaise," Brad thought quickly, "somewhere easy, in the open Le Lavandou, there is a large bar, Bar Restaurant Mariniere opposite the Marina. Four o'clock." Brad added allowing time for Falaise to get there. Without argument Falaise agreed, repeating the location and time.

"Please be there M'sieu, it is very urgent!"

Brad grunted, "I'll be there." he hung up.

"Well, what do you know," grinned Greg, really

pouting wonder what's put the breeze up his baggy pants?"

Brad decided to delay contacting Dubois until after the meeting, much to Brigitte's disapproval.

"You should take Dubois with you," she said crossly, "let him get the information." Brad pacified her by agreeing to take Greg and to contact Dubois immediately after they had met Falaise. Four o'clock found them both sipping a beer in the Bar Mariniere. A group of French locals were intent on playing 'boules,' along the gravel area edging the main road, the myriad of yachts and boats shimmering in the hot sun swaying slightly in the gentle swell of the harbour. Jacques Falaise was early his small Renault 5 drew up edging into the herringbone parking facing the ocean, his fat and hairy figure immediately recognizable. Brad was convinced he still had the same ill-fitting trousers as he had on before, sagging at the rear, constantly being hitched up with elbow and thumbs.

He walked quickly across the roadway looking warily around. Seeing Brad he hurried across, relief on his face. He offered his hand. Both Brad and Greg ignored it.

"What do you want Falaise?" Brad was brusque, his face hard Falaise glanced nervously around him, "I find this very difficult to say," he said quietly mopping his forehead with a grimy handkerchief.

"Not half as difficult as we find it to listen to, if you don't say something," grunted Greg.

Falaise looked startled at Greg's fluent French. "You have heard of the murder of Hans Kleiber?" Jacques kept his voice low, his eyes watching to see no one was near enough to be overheard.

"Thought you didn't know him?" Brad's tone was sardonic.

Falaise gestured apologetically, "As I said I was not myself. A man came to see me, threatened me, smashed a very valuable glass ornament," his eyes saddened, "I had to tell him where Kleiber was, you know the man I mean." He looked at Brad who said nothing, "soon afterwards Kleiber was killed it was in the papers now perhaps it will be Karl Brandt."

"Who...?" Greg sat up, glancing at Brad. This was the first time another name had ever been mentioned. "Who did you say?"

Karl Brandt he was another of the men on the boat, the other one who hired it from me." Falaise was careful to avoid any suggestion of them being anything other than clients. "He owns a Garage in Nimes they have both hired a boat before for their holiday."

"Hold it right there." Greg got to his feet, face set, eyes narrowing as he combed his mind. "I'll be right back."

Brad was startled, Greg set off towards the 'Maison de la Presse' quickly and purposefully. After a few minutes he returned carrying two newspapers. He sat down rapidly turning the large sheets which flapped irritatingly in the breeze.

"Ah," Greg folded back the paper and read quickly, "I thought so, thought I read this earlier, listen... The body of a man was recovered yesterday by police divers from the sea near San F'eliu des Guixols, Spain. His car had been seen to plunge 200 metres from the coast road after striking an obstruction. An eye witness described the accident. The car was being driven very fast there was no chance of avoiding the rocks in the road. Attempts are being made to recover the car. The man was later identified as being Karl Brandt, a German National part owner of a Garage and used car business in Nimes. Police are continuing the investigation."

"Is that him?" Greg looked up at Falaise, Jacques had gone white. He nodded swallowing. "mon Dieu' what is to become of us?"

"No suggestion that Brandt was murdered," said Greg, "seems to have run out of road and hit the rocks."

"It says he was driving very very fast," mused Brad, "I wonder why?" He said no more anxious not to give away too much to Falaise until he had learned more. "You'd better tell us everything Falaise," he growled ominously, "I'm beginning to realise you know a damned sight more than you admit."

Jacques Falaise was in a panic. He had no doubt the Mafia were behind the death of Brandt, now it was Pierre, they would be after Pierre now.

"Do you know how we can call off this murderer

M'sieu Carter," he said, eyes Beseeching, "please before he can kill again."

Both Brad and Greg were astonished at the desperation in the man, what was with him that these people had been murdered, even if they had been friends, it was hardly grounds for such fear inspired begging.

Brad began to see the light, "who is the other man Falaise?" he asked quietly, "who is the other one you don't want killed."

"I want to make a deal with you..."

"No deals, nothing, unless you tell us everything," Brad snapped.

Falaise collapsed he hung his head clasping his hands between his knees.

"My son," he said without looking up, "the other man is my son. I don't want him to die, he did nothing to the girl he just did, well did nothing. Perhaps he should have done, but he didn't." He lifted his face and looked tragically at Brad, his eyes brimming. "Please stop this man, you were the one who must have sent him, you can stop him killing my boy. I will do any-thing, pay anything, you can have everything I have got, please..."

"Goddamn," muttered Greg visibly shaken, "Goddamn!"

Brad was not surprised at the information it should have been obvious. The unnecessary antagonism of

Falaise at first which showed a more personal involvement, the desperation to contact him believing the assassinations were Brad's responsibility, which they were, he thought bitterly, the beseeching attitude, his own son for Christ sake. Brad took a deep breath.

"I can't stop it now," he said softly, more to himself than Falaise.

Falaise looked up startled, "but it was you who started everything, I thought ...."

Brad glared at him. "The woman I loved was raped and murdered! Thrown into the sea, destroyed for nothing! Nothing and you expect me to do something. They deserved what they got all of them, your son too! Spineless little bastard even if he didn't help to kill her, why should I help you or him." He broke off his attempts to convince himself unsuccessful.

Falaise was stricken, he had felt sure that pleading with Carter would lift the threat that hung over his son, not considering the possibility that he would refuse to help. Brad looked at him belligerently, detesting him, contempt in his eyes.

"The only chance you have Falaise is to bring your son to the police, he must tell them everything, if he did nothing they will take that into consideration at least that will save him from being slaughtered like the others." Without waiting for Falaise to reply he went on, "Where is he now, your son," Brad pulled out the rolled sketch becoming creased and dog eared by now and spread it in front of the distressed Frenchman. "Is this him?"

'Brad pointed to the younger features. Falaise nodded miserably, "merde!"

Carter has a copy of the picture there was no hope, everyone was after Pierre.

"Where is he?" insisted Brad.

Falaise shrugged. "I don't know," he muttered miserably, "he went to Toulon I think. I haven't heard from him since."

"Where in Toulon?" asked Greg.

"I don't know, he knows no one there, it was just that he had to get away after the mafia came looking."

Brads eyes narrowed, "so it was this little bastard who gave away Kleibers whereabouts. Well we had better find him quick smart," grunted Brad, "before they do, I'll tell the police, tell them everything, perhaps they can find your son, what's his name?"

"Pierre?" Falaise said, his hopes rising, the police were better than the Mafia. Anyone was better than the Mafia. He peered gratefully at Brad and Greg.

"Who else knows what went on," Brads' eyes narrowed, "what took place on the boat."

"Only Pierre," Falaise mopped his streaming face. "With Kleiber and Brandt dead, Pierre told me everything when he returned, but I have told no one."

"What about that blonde in your office?"

Falaise shook his head. "She knows something is wrong, I told her not to talk about Kleiber or Brandt that was all, she doesn't know what took place."

Brad nodded obviously the assassin couldn't have known Pierre was involved when he terrified Falaise.

"The only reason I'm doing this is because I don't approve of the continued killing, but that son of yours is still as guilty as the other two. I don't really give a damn whether he lives or dies as long as he is caught, so don't get any false impressions Falaise."

He scribbled Greg's telephone number on a piece of paper and slid it across the table.

"Find him somehow and then ring me there immediately do as I say and don't try anything devious and perhaps we can save him from being sliced up." Falaise shuddered. "If you do he must take his chances."

Falaise nodded, starting to effuse his gratitude, but Brad's face stopped him. He stood up and hurried back to his car his trousers flapping. Brad looked at Greg as Falalise drove away.

"What a jar of worms all this is," he said, "what sort of animal have I let loose for Christ's sake."

Greg looked sympathetic, "they deserved what they got Brad" he, said quietly, "you weren't to know what would happen to them, even if Pierre gets knocked off, he's just as bad."

"That's not the point now Greg I feel just as guilty as the bastard who sliced up Kleiber, and who obviously had something to do with Brandt diving off the cliff. I have to save this lad's life. Not because he's worth it, but just to redeem what I've done. I can't have his murder on my conscience as well, I couldn't live with it. I must find him, for my own sake."

Greg looked at Brad, sad to see the drawn and haggard features, the deep pain in his eyes. Goddamn... he thought, Goddamn. He ordered two beers.

Chapter 19

They drove straight to Nice, joining the autoroute and arriving just before 4pm. Inspector Dubois was waiting, hopeful and expectantly, Brad having rung before they left. Dubois was congratulating himself on his wisdom in leaving Brad time to think and contemplate things through. Now Dubois hoped matters would revert to their rightful structure.

He listened attentively, taking copious notes, avoiding criticism either in his occasional questions or his manner. There would be time enough to examine Brads actions later. Now was the time to put a stop to the rollercoaster of violence. He was astonished to read the news report of Brandt. That was news to him, Brad and Greg related everything. Dubois pursed his lips. Perhaps, just perhaps, this was the break he was waiting for.

Dubois immediately circulated the description of Pierre, adding emphasis to the situation. The sparse description of Packer was also circulated. Little was known of him except from Falaise. The number of the Peugeot being driven by Pierre held the most hope. The Toulon Police would spot that said Dubois confidently. It was late when they arrived home, drained by the interview, depressed by the whole sordid business. Brigitte was worried, she wisely hid her anxiety as they appeared and poured three stiff whiskies, allowing time before asking the thousand questions which ate into her. She prepared a quick meal and listened, nodding in agreement as everything unfolded.

"Thank God," she breathed as they finished, "now you can leave it all to the police, what a shame it took so long for you to realise, never mind you'll feel better Brad." Brad nodded, not believing her. It had after all been him who'd put out the contract.

Pierre was quite content staying with Marie Louise was a new and delightful experience. She fussed over him, bringing food home from work and producing a variety of dishes from the small kitchenette, happy that she was on shift work, which meant either mornings or long evenings and nights with Pierre. She wasn't going to let him get away easily she had decided and insisted that he didn't go out until things were quieter. Pierre contented himself with television and books whilst Marie Louise worked and told her how lonely he had been when she returned. Marie Louise wasn't slow to dissipate his loneliness with affection and passion between the sheets of the creaking bed. Pierre's fears quietened and were almost forgotten, but he mentioned Karl to Marie Louise.

"I should try and find out where he is, at least tell him what's happened, my father too, he should know where I am he'll be worried. On top of that I should know if anything else has happened."

"You are not going out yet?" Marie Louise was

emphatic. "If you like I will ring Yvonne and tell her you are ok and see if there is a message from Karl."

Pierre thought for a moment and then nodded, that would do no harm, and his father would be relieved. If Karl had rung he could slip out when Marie Louise was at work and ring him. Marie Louise rang the next morning. Yvonne was both delighted and surprised to hear from Marie Louise, even more surprised when Marie Louise asked if there were any messages for Pierre.

"What do you know about Pierre?" asked Yvonne, "I didn't think you had seen him since the disco?"

Marie Louise chuckled and told Yvonne they were staying together, "Pierre wants to tell his Papa that he is safe, ok and happy," she added sexily.

"Well," laughed Yvonne, "The sly dog, I didn't know he had it in him. I don't know what's been going on, seems that no one's supposed to know where anyone else is these days."

Marie Louise decided not to say anything about Pierre's affairs he had told her to say nothing.

"Give him my love," said Yvonne, "I'll tell his dad that he's safe and sound. Nothing has happened here, the old man doesn't tell me anything but he's like a crazy man lately, frightened of his own shadow." She hung up.

Jacques Falaise didn't appear at the office that day. He left early for Toulon intending to scour the streets for Pierre. He couldn't think where to look, perhaps he would spot the car, see him in one of the bars. He was not sure whether he had done the right thing by informing Carter. The only reason was that he had hoped Carter would call off the assassin, believing Pierre to be innocent of the girl's death, but now it meant the Police being involved. Police and the Mafia, oil and water they didn't mix somehow. The thought of Pierre languishing in a prison cell for years seemed a poor substitute. Perhaps if Pierre went far away, somewhere safe until the whole thing died down. There was no sign of the Peugeot, side streets and car parks revealed nothing. He drove slowly through the underground parking lots, scoured the less popular bars and cafes. Frustrated and weary Falaise turned for home. Pierre may well have gone further than Toulon, there was no telling where he was, it meant waiting for a letter or phone call he would have to get in touch the money wouldn't last for ever. As long as that murdering bastard didn't find him first, his stomach churned at the thought. The next morning Falaise arrived early at the boatyard, searching Yvonne's desk and his own for signs of a message. There was nothing.

Yvonne arrived late which had done nothing for Falaise's state of mind. "Where the hell have you been?"

"Car wouldn't start, took me ages to find someone." Yvonne slung her bag under the desk and settled herself.

"Time you got rid of that wreck," grumbled Jacques, "It's falling apart."

"If you paid me a decent wage I could afford to," retorted Yvonne. She got up, and sauntered across to make some coffee. "Pierre phoned," she said brightly.

"What, when, when did he phone?"

"Last night just before I went home..."

"You didn't tell me," Falaise was angry but relieved.

"You weren't here were you? Anyway he's ok. He didn't actually phone, it was his girlfriend."

"What girl-friend, he hasn't got a bloody girlfriend."

Yvonne grinned, sugaring her coffee. "He has now they're living together in Toulon."

"Where, where in Toulon...?" Yvonne told him the address and the rest of the conversation with Marie Louise. Falaise hunted into his office.

"Don't you dare tell anyone else where Pierre is," he shouted over his shoulder. "no one, not a bloody soul or I'll break your neck."

Yvonne slumped sullenly in her chair. 'Tipped on me bum, treated like garbage, now he wants to break me neck. Christ what a life she sipped her coffee sullenly. Jacques Falaise was in turmoil of indecision now he knew where to find Pierre. Should he phone Carter, he'd promised to do so, but what would Carter do, fetch the Police? They would all descend on Pierre like dogs on a rabbit. No, he would find Pierre himself first, see what the boy said, try and work something out. Carter didn't want to help, just to salve his own conscience. Sod

174

Carter.

Falaise hurried out of the office. "I probably won't be back," he said, "don't forget what I said..."

Yvonne stuck her tongue out at his retreating back. Good riddance she thought. Jacques Falaise didn't return to the office, he didn't even reach Toulon, not in the way he had expected to. Desperate to find Pierre he drove fast and belligerently, irritable at the slow moving traffic he overtook impatiently, snaking through gaps and openings, careless of speed limits, snarling away from traffic lights, rubber smearing the road.

The road narrowed ahead forcing him to join the slow moving vehicles he fretted, peering around the car ahead. The road widened into three lanes. Jacques swung out and gunned the engine. The Renault leapt away past the line, engine howling. He changed into top gear and raced along the centre lane. He was nearly at the head of the line when an Opel, being driven impatiently in the other direction overtook and appeared in the centre lane on a collision course. The Opel was too far out to recover position, Jacques wrenched frantically at the wheel swerving viciously to the right missing the leading car by inches. The Opel ripped by. The Renault swung, the force throwing the rear end to and throw he struggled to correct the snaking car. Panic causing him to overcompensate, the car staggered and slithered, the front wheel digging into the roadside ditch, deep into gravel. The front of the car stopped suddenly, the back end surging upwards twisting and turning into the tangled undergrowth. Mangled the Renault struck a tree and stopped its mad gyrations, steam hissing from a fractured radiator, one wheel spinning grotesquely on a broken axle. Jacques head slammed into the windscreen, miraculously unbroken, wipers flicking madly.

Pierre jumped as the doorbell shrilled. His heart lurched. Who was that, Marie Louise was working until 9 pm. she had her own key anyway. No one else knew he was there. He stood up, "Who is it he called.

"Telegram, urgent, M'sieu Falaise...?"

Pierre hesitated, not wanting to open the door, worried, anxious to know. "Slide it under the door."

"You must sign," said the voice irritably.

"When I see it..."

A light blue envelope appeared silently beneath the ill-fitting door. Pierre picked it up, it was authentic enough. He flicked the double lock and opened the door. A small disinterested Postman bag slung across his shoulder, offered a dog eared pad and chewed pencil. Pierre scrawled a signature and locked the door quickly. He ripped open the envelope.

"Father injured car accident. Genre Hospital Generale Toulon. Yvonne."

Pierre sagged, his father injured, how bad was he, please God he's not dead. How had that happened, in Toulon? The possibility of the accident being associated with everything else crossed his mind, had they tried to kill his father as well. Pierre sat down, sick and unhappy. He must go to his father at once. He collected keys and money and scribbled a note for Marie Louise in case he needed to stay. Shrugging on his jacket he let himself out of the apartment, his ears alert looking at shadows. He ran down the stairs and hurried through a dingy alleyway, which led on to a building site, the ground covered with debris. The Peugeot sat inconspicuously beside a corrugated workman's hut. Pierre drove carefully away across the site on to the muddy and rough side road.

Packer woke early, his head muzzy, mouth dry. He looked with distaste at the naked girl asleep on her stomach next to him, exhausted. He slapped her bare backside and pitting his foot against her hip shoved her out of the bed. She fell in a tangle of sheets, a stream of French invective pouring from her rouge smudged lips. Packer threw some money at her and lit a cigarette.

"Get out," he muttered thickly. The girl gathered up the notes and pulled on her clothes. Still mouthing obscenities she hurried out of the room slamming the door behind her. Packer showered and dressed. Two scalding cups of coffee later he climbed in to the Audi and headed for Marseilles. There was still some unfinished business to attend to. Pierre arrived at the hospital a bundle of nerves. Worried about how he would find his father, his senses at screaming point seeing sudden death in every darkened corner and suspicious vehicle. He hurried into the main foyer and enquired at the desk.

"Jacques Falaise, he was injured in a car accident. I'm not sure when. I am his son, I have only just heard."

The Nurse smiled sympathetically. This happened so frequently. Families worried about victims on the road who kept the wards filled with broken bodies. She sighed to herself and checked the records.

"Third floor Dr. Neissler's Ward, your father is in room 319."

Pierre nodded and hurried to the lifts. It seemed an interminable time before the doors clattered open. He stepped in and pressed the button. He walked quickly through the swing doors, offices, toilets, room number 312. He searched along the corridor. 319. Fearfully he opened the door slowly, frightened of what he may find.

Jacques Falaise was lying, propped against a pile of pillows his head swathed in white bandages. Both eyes were black and his nose puffy and swollen. He peered painfully at Pierre as the door opened.

"Papa...?" Pierre wasn't sure. He looked as though he had been hit with a bulldozer.

"Pierre..." Falaise was astonished to see his son. Very relieved he tried to smile but the effort was too painful.

Pierre realised that the injuries were not too serious. "How are you? What happened?" he pointed to the bandages. "Your head...?"

"Concussion they say, nothing serious, got to stay

here for 2 days. Damned fools, bandaging me up like a Maypole. They don't know how hard my head is."

Pierre smiled to himself, he knew.

Jacques described the accident managing to blame everything, except himself. "Forced off the road," he lied, "only travelling slowly bloody steering was dodgy."

Pierre listened assessing for himself the causes. He knew his father very well. Thank God he was ok.

A nurse entered carrying a tray of hypodermic syringes and a range of phials. "Time for your shot M'sieu," she beamed brightly. Falaise scowled and wriggled his ample rear out of the sheets. The Nurse gaily jabbed in the needle and squeezed the plunger. "Merci," she moved on.

"Sadists," muttered Jacques rubbing his buttock. "Love it they do, rushing around like butterfly collectors, sticking everything they see. Doesn't bother them I'm laying here like a mashed cat."

Pierre decided there was nothing much wrong with the old man. He told his father where he was, how lucky he had been to meet up with Marie Louise, "Nothing to worry about as long as I stay out of sight."

"You can't do that for ever," said Jacques. "you know Brandt's dead?"

Pierre's mouth dropped open. "No, I hadn't heard, what happened."

"Flew off a cliff in Spain smashed to bits at the

179

bottom he is."

"Murdered?" Breathed Pierre shocked. "Jacques shrugged, and wished he hadn't he blinked head hurting.

"No idea... Things are getting hot. You're not safe shacked up in Toulon, the moment you show your nose this bastard will shoot it off. You'll have to get away, north coast, Switzerland. I don't know somewhere until things are quieter."

"I can't, where can I go? I've got no money, know nobody, besides there's Marie Louise now," he finished lamely.

Jacque face turned red with anger. With his white bandages, blue black eyes and his red cheeks he was certainly Patriotic, thought Pierre, looks like the tricolour.

"Marie Louise," he roared, bringing his voice down as the nurse glared at him, "knickers to Marie Louise, you can find a bit of the other anywhere if that's what you want. What are you going to do get blown away for a bit of ass!"

The Nurse walked to the bedside and looked at them both sternly. "You are supposed to be resting M'sieu. If you don't settle down I must ask your visitor to leave." She frowned at Pierre and waggled her wrist, "It's not visiting time you know, you shouldn't be here until 7 pm."

Jacques Falaise quietened down, "Listen," he tried to

lean forward, his head throbbed he beckoned to Pierre who drew his chair closer. "Go back to the office, tell that stupid Vache Yvonne you want some money out of the safe. You'd better take 10,000 euros."

Pierre's eyes widened, he didn't know his father kept so much cash on hand. Jacques interpreted his expression.

"Must hang on to some," he muttered, bloody taxes, Government would take the lot if they could."

"Take 10,000, as a loan," he added knowing there was a fat chance of ever seeing it again, go to Corsica."

"How for God's sake," spluttered Pierre.

"On a bloody boat you fool," growled Falaise, "how do you think, it's too deep to paddle. The boats go from Marseilles to Ajaccio the place will be full of tourists laying in the sun like rotten sheep. If you don't live it up like some rock star you'll be alright for months. You could even get a job..." Jacques didn't look as though he thought that likely. "Give me a ring when you find somewhere to stay, tell me where you are and I'll cover here for you when they let me out of this bone market." He added spitefully. "Now sod off and look after yourself." His eyes softened in the discoloured puffiness.

"Pierre looked at him." Anything you want, books, food...?"

Jacques grinned... "Bit of embrocation for me arse."

Pierre left, grateful that his father would be none the

worse for wear in a few days and hurried to the car. As Pierre drove towards Marseilles, relieved to have found his father relatively unscathed the anxieties of his own circumstances began to eat into him. He couldn't just disappear to Corsica, there was Marie Louise now. They had grown very fond of each other she had unselfishly helped him when he most needed help, trusting him. He couldn't abandon her now, besides he loved her, loved her bright happiness, loved her for loving him, no one had ever cared about him as she did. He looked at his watch, 5.30 another three and a half hours before Marie Louise left work. He would collect the money and wait for her to come home before he did anything. Worried in case Yvonne left work before he arrived Pierre pulled the car over at the next telephone box and dialled. Yvonne answered.

"Did you get the telegram?" Yvonne asked.

"Yes, I've been to see Papa, he's not too bad, his eyes are black and he has a bit of concussion. He should be out in a few days. I need some money, he told me to take some from the safe. Can you wait until I arrive, I'll only be half an hour or so."

"Bien sur," Yvonne agreed, "Is it safe for you to come here."

"I must, after that I am clearing off for a while. Keep your eyes open, this bastard is still after me, you know the one I mean."

Yvonne remembered her bruised behind vividly. "Do

you think he will be back?" She sounded very anxious, with Jacques in hospital she was on her own, she didn't fancy another visit.

"I don't know?" Replied Pierre, "Just watch out for him, give me the tip if you see anything..."

Yvonne said she would. More anxious than ever, "hurry up then," she hung up.

Pierre arrived just after 6 pm. and hurried up the stairs into the office. He had driven cautiously into the Yard his eyes flicking anxiously. Nothing seemed different. Yvonne was pleased to see him. She had never really thought a lot about Pierre but now felt sorry for him, he wasn't such a bad sort. She wanted to help. Opening the safe she passed over the money, grinning at Pierre's face when he saw the amount of cash his father had secreted away.

"He knows every euro that's here, won't put it in the bank says his money is his business, if the bloody place caught fire..."

"Where are you off to, whatever are you going to do with yourself?"

"I'm off to Corsica, but for Christ's sake don't tell anyone. Papa thinks I can hide out there for a while, better than the mainland, it's busy with holidaymakers."

Yvonne looked dubious, "Marie Louise, how about her?"

"I don't know, I haven't seen her yet, she's working

until 9. I hope she'll come with me." Pierre didn't seem to sure.

Yvonne's face softened, "Like that is it between you two. Go on clear off, give us a ring and take care."

She reached up and kissed Pierre, watched him as he climbed into the Peugeot and drove away. She sighed and locked the office door. Marie Louise had hurried home, she hated these late shifts, seemed to take up the whole day, by the time she reached the apartment there wasn't much of an evening left. She let herself in and called cheerily to Pierre. She hugged him and kissed him fondly. His eyes showed concern something was wrong, she could detect that at once.

Pierre had fretted, waiting for her, worrying about the whole damned business, he didn't want to go to Corsica, didn't want to lose Marie Louise but didn't want to be slaughtered either. He told Marie Louise what had happened as she started to prepare a meal. She listened carefully anxious about his father, nodding when Pierre told her about the money and Corsica.

"I just don't know what to do," he sighed unhappily, "everything is so mixed up."

"Corsica is a very good idea," she said firmly, "we can leave first thing tomorrow the ferry leaves at 8 am."

Pierre looked at her amazed. "You'll come with me you really will come with me?" He couldn't hide the relief in his voice.

"What about your job, your flat and everything. I

can't ask you to give all that up."

Marie Louise smiled. "The rent is paid until the end of the month, I can lock everything up, that's no problem, and I'll tell them at work that something urgent has come up. I'm due for two weeks holiday anyway. They can manage without me. When we get settled we can see what turns up."

She walked over to Pierre and put her arms around his neck, kneeling in front of him. Her big eyes looked at him softly. "Trouble is I think I love you," she said quietly, "I don't much care what happens as long as it happens to us both." She kissed him hard and long Pierre pulled her close. She wriggled away giggling, "food first, nourishment later."

Chapter 20

Packer arrived in Marseilles. His only lead now was the boatyard, he had no doubt Pierre Falaise had disappeared by this time. Be no problem to find him, just put the fear of God into his fat father and take it from there. Packer didn't much relish the idea of exposing himself to Falaise again, the fat fool may well panic and talk to the wrong people, Packers safety depended on anonymity, the fewer who saw him, the less chance of him being remembered. However, it couldn't be avoided this time, he cursed himself for not realising the third man was the son of Falaise it would have been so much easier if he had known, so much safer.

Packer left his Hotel at 9 am and drove slowly to the 'Ghantier Pegasus. For a while he sat in the Audi and watched. The yard murmured with machinery and a few people came and went to the office. All seemed normal. Picking his opportunity when everything was calm he walked swiftly across to the stairs and mounted them silently. He opened the office door and reached for Yvonne before she realised anyone had entered.

Yvonne looked up, her face blanched, her mouth opening to scream.

"Shut up," snarled Packer, the look on his face

enough to stifle the unuttered shriek of panic in Yvonne's throat. Yvonne had tried to remember details of Packer's appearance without too much success, seeing him suddenly appear in front of her, her brain immediately recognised him. She shrank back in the chair terrified.

"Where's Falaise, young Falaise, just tell me and you won't get hurt." Packer perched on the end of the desk and looked at her hard. She felt so alone there was no one she could call to for help.

"I don't know," she managed to get out.

"Liar," replied Packer cheerfully, "try again last chance," he picked up a paper knife and toyed with it.

"He's in Toulon somewhere," Yvonne's brain raced. By this time Pierre would be gone, probably half way to Corsica. Certainly well out of the way by the time this creep reached Toulon. It would do no harm to tell. If she could get rid of him perhaps she could think of something.

Packer's eyes narrowed. "Where in Toulon..."

"With a friend, an apartment, rue la Magdalen. I don't know the number."

"Friend, what sort of friend?"

"His girlfriend, they're living together, I don't know her name."

"Where's the boss?" Packer jerked his head towards the inner door.

"Out..." Yvonne answered nervously. "I don't know where he is either." She wasn't going to mention the hospital it would mean admitting she was really on her own.

Packer stood up and leaned over the desk, Yvonne felt her head flutter.

"If that's the truth you won't see me, if it isn't and I don't find Falaisie I know where I can find you young lady!"

Packer stood and leaned towards Yvonne, her heart fluttered. He drew the paper knife across his throat significantly. Packer then walked out. He didn't look back. Yvonne sank in her chair with relief. She felt sick.

It took Yvonne ten minutes to recover from the shock, now that she had given away Pierre's previous whereabouts she was less certain. Perhaps he hadn't left yet, may still be at the apartment. In the anxiety of the moment it had seemed the best thing to do. Now she wasn't so sure. If only the old man was here. He wasn't exactly a pillar of strength but at least he could do something. There was no one. No one she could ask, talk to call on to help. Falaise had rung someone when he had been threatened by this bugger before, who was that, Carter, the one who came first. He was nice, seemed to be anyway. Perhaps he would help. Yvonne got up and searched the file. The card was there, Paris telephone number. She made a cup of coffee, unsure, wanting to do the right thing by Pierre, right by herself. The thought of the knife sliding across her own throat decided her, someone had to stamp on this creature. She dialled.

Mac picked up the phone and listened. Brad had assured him there was no reason to avoid giving out his present whereabouts. He told Yvonne the number in St. Aygulf.

Brigitte answered. "Is M'sieu Carter there please," Yvonne was cautious.

"No, not at the moment," Brigitte didn't recognize the voice, "Who's speaking?"

"I'm the secretary of M'sieu Falaise, in Marseilles, could you tell me when M'sieu Carter will he back please."

"Is it about his son?" Yvonne was startled. She hadn't expected such a blunt response.

She stammered, "well yes, in a way, who is that...?"

Brigitte sensed the insecurity in Yvonne, and injected friendliness in her voice, didn't want the girl hanging up in fright, there may be something here that would help.

"I know all about this awful business, and just like M'sieu Carter I want to help. Help to find Pierre, is there anything you can tell me or anything we can do to help you?" Brigitte added, her intuition telling her Yvonne was scared.

Yvonne responded to Brigitte, the offer to help washed over her. She needed help that was why she had phoned, irrespective of the reaction she would get from

Carter. This woman was different She sounded concerned, Showed understanding. Yvonne talked to her, warming to the replies explaining all that had taken place, she felt her fears fading, "I'm so frightened Madame Carter," she finished.

"I'm not Madame Carter," laughed Brigitte, "I'm married to another nice guy, call me Brigitte." Brigitte's questions had revealed that Yvonne didn't really know the whole background to the rotten business. She had been caught up in the skirts of the violence.

"Exactly where is Pierre now?" asked Brigitte.

"I don't really know," said Yvonne helplessly, "the last I knew he was leaving early for Corsica, but I don't know if he has gone. Now this bloody creep is on his way to Toulon. If Pierre is still there..." she broke off miserably.

"If you can I feel you should get out of there." Brigitte became brisk and business like, "M'sieu Carter and my husband should be back here soon, we will meet you in Toulon. See if we can find Pierre before this murderer does. We can tell you everything that's happened then. Besides you'll be safer away from the office, in case he comes back."

"Meet you at the ferry in Toulon, how about 1pm?" Yvonne agreed readily. 'Won't hurt to shut this dump up for a while," she said, 'how will I know you? I've only seen M'sieu Carter once?"

"It will be difficult to miss us. My husband is built like

190

a Jumbo Jet." Brigitte hung up, fretting.

Brad and Greg had gone off to Greg's office to seek out any extra information that may not have been published. She put the kettle on and changed her mind pouring a stiff Gin and Tonic instead. Brigitte contemplated telling the Police, she was not at all sure that Brad would do so. Both he and Greg were too concerned with finding Pierre themselves. Half the trouble was Greg. Ever since this whole thing started he had fancied himself as an amateur Sherlock Holmes. The two of them rushing round like a pair of spaniels that had lost a bone. She grinned Greg, was rather like a spaniel, big eyes, loving. She felt a flood of affection, and just as bloody daft. She swallowed some Gin.

Perhaps she had better wait until they came in. Brad would be angry if she jumped the gun. She set her lips. "Ok but I shall make sure he tells Dubois immediately. No more 'Do it yourself' nonsense. She poured another Gin. 'This stuff could catch on,' she decided. It was almost an hour later that Brad and Greg returned. Brigitte was getting anxious there was not a lot of time to meet Yvonne. She greeted Gregg with a curtsy.

"Doctor Watson I presume," she said gravely and flounced merrily into the lounge.

Greg looked at her suspiciously. "You been on the sauce?' he grunted.

"Sauce... sauce was invented by the French to cover their mistakes. Rather like putting on new boots to hide your laddered tights. Yvonne phoned," she added.

"Yvonne? Who the hell is Yvonne? Greg asked.

"Brad knows, don't you Brad?" Brad looked blank and shook his head.

"Yvonne," said Brigitte in a conspiratorial tone, "is the secretary to fatty Falaise." she waited for effect. "She knows where Pierre is."

They both looked interested, "Where?" Brad was eager, "Come on Brigitte don't muck about."

"Pierre has been tucked up in Toulon with his latest little chocolate drop, but is now on his way to Corsica, would you believe."

Brigitte became serious and outlined her conversation with Yvonne. 'We have to meet Yvonne in Toulon, by the ferry at 1. It is now," Brigitte peered at her watch the face seemed a bit blurred, "11.45 am so we must get going."

"What's this we business," asked Greg, "you're not coming! It's too bloody dangerous anyway, you're sloshed."

"I most certainly am not, and I am most certainly going," said Brigitte haughtily, Greg blinked and looked hopelessly at Brad. Brad grinned. Brigitte was like a burst of sunlight.

Brigitte placed her hands firmly on her hips, her chin jutting.

"Ring Dubois, Brad," she said firmly, "tell him everything. Let's get this in the hands of the right people."

"We'll see Yvonne first, see whether..."

"No more, firsts, Brad. Brigitte was firmly ready for an argument. "This whole thing looks like a crooked horse race already, every horse coming first except the winner. You ring Dubois now, no more delays."

Brad capitulated, glancing at Greg who raised his eyebrows he knew from experience that when Brigitte made up her mind nothing would change it, not even logic, least of all logic.

Brad asked to be put through to Inspector Dubois.

The Inspector had been keeping a low profile. He admitted to himself that he was less interested in the two dead men than he was in associating the killings with Don Vittorino. a chance of connecting him with murder would ensure the courts putting the mafia cape out of circulation for a long time to come. Clearing up the empire he controlled would be far easier once Vittorino lost the reins. Consequently Dubois was prepared to wait, unwilling to allow false leads to misguide the final pounce. He listened attentively to Brad Carter.

"It would appear M'sieu Carter that the young lady you are about to meet would have a very good idea of the possible murderers description. If that is so, I would appreciate it if you would let me have full details. If I can secure this man's arrest and subsequent investigation we can, perhaps, get him out of the picture. In which case young Falaise will be safe, assuming that is," he added drily, "that you have changed your mind about arranging his demise."

"You know my feelings about that Inspector," snapped Brad, "It is only to see justice done that I am concerned at all. I no longer wish him dead. In fact I am surprised that the Toulon Police have been unable to trace him by now, seeing that he has been in Toulon all the time." Dubois said nothing.

"I must again remind you that to interfere with the course of justice is a serious matter. Please, if you learn anything, seek the local police assistance. I shall look forward to hearing from you hopefully with a description of the man who has threatened the young lady." Dubois hung up.

"There you are," said Brad looking at Brigitte, "Doesn't want to know. Quite prepared to let us do all the dirty work, and then step in to take the credit."

"You can't expect him to arrive as soon as you snap your fingers." Brigitte had been listening on the extension earpiece. "He can't fly up and down the Riviera, like a leaf in a March wind. He has a lot to look after."

Brigitte was secretly disappointed that Dubois hadn't dropped everything and rushed to help. She wasn't happy at all about Brad and Greg snooping about with a murderer loose.

After an argument between Greg and Brigitte who insisted on coming, finally won by Greg who pointed out that Gabrielle needed picking up from nursery school at 3 pm. they set off for Toulon, promising not to take any chances and to contact Brigitte as soon as they could. Greg seemed preoccupied as they drove to Toulon, his face solemn. Brad glanced at him, Greg was usually buoyant company.

"What are your feelings about this guy Pierre?" he suddenly asked.

Brad was surprised at the question, "You know what they are. I hate the little cretin. At first I wanted him as dead as the others, but not now. Not after seeing what violence was involved. I don't want to see him carved up. But I want him slung inside for years."

"How'd you reckon that's going to be achieved, assuming we find him?"

Brad was puzzled. "All that we have to do is keep this murdering menace off his back and hand him over to the police. I'm just desperate to save his life ironical isn't it?" Brad laughed without humour, "what are you getting at Greg?"

"What I'm getting at is that I don't think you've got a snowflakes chance in hell of getting him put away. Dubois isn't interested in Pierre. He knows there's no evidence against him. No case to answer, no way he could make the charges stick. Dubois wants one person, Vittorino, not Kleiber, not Brandt, not Pierre... Vittorino that's who he has always been after, he's using you for that reason."

Brad was shocked, "rubbish," he snorted, "Pierre's as guilty as the others and Dubois knows it."

"Alright," Greg went on doggedly emphasising his points on his fingers. "If Pierre denies everything what case is there? One, he admits that Michelle went aboard to do the sketch, but she left again. No one saw her go to sea not even Andre, remember he was in the bar when the boat left. Two, Michelle is found at Cannes... nothing to indicate where she was thrown overboard, raped and assaulted, but no other motive. The only witnesses who could involve Pierre are dead. If he denies everything, he's home free."

Brad was shocked, "Falaise knows bloody well what happened, pretty sure that he didn't actually kill Michelle, but Brandt or Kleiber did and that makes him as bad."

"Circumstantial," grunted Greg.

"His father knows, Pierre told him and Falaise told us."

"Hearsay evidence, inadmissible, anyway can you imagine the old man helping to crucify his own son?"

"He's running, panicked, that shows he has something to hide."

"Could be anything... Women, all of us are either running away from them, or after them. Fact of Life..."

Brad was worried. What Greg was saying meant he was laying himself open for nothing, meant Pierre escaping the retribution which had resulted in Brad becoming as guilty as the others.

Greg went on, "Dubois wants the murderer of Kleiber, call him Joe Bloggs, not just because he killed Kleiber, but because he did it for Vittorino and for you." Greg grimaced at Brad, "If he gets Joe Bloggs, he gets Vittorino and that's what he wants. End of story, except that if Vittorino tumbles you will tumble too. Dubois needs you, needs to convict you in order to wipe out the Vittorino menace. You are in trouble my friend," Greg added grimly, "there is only one small light in all this mess. Pierre must confess in writing. Incriminate the others admit his own fear and impotence which stopped him from helping. It won't get you off the hook but it would help, you'd be dangling by your shirt tail instead of by your wedding tackle, as you are now."

Brad stared ahead. Greg was right. It explained the apparent lack of interest of Dubois. Explained why he'd been left to do the donkey work Dubois was waiting. Waiting for the Mafia Hit man! If Pierre was blown away, too bad, it gave more chance to find the man who could tie in Don Vittorino.

"Christ." Brad swore.

Chapter 21

Marie Louise was up early, showered and dressed in tight jeans and a gay sloppy jumper. An overnight case packed with clothes was all she would need for her holiday. She chattered incessantly and happily. She'd never been to Corsica, never been on a real holiday, especially with a man. She bubbled over, the ominous overhanging reasons lost in her excitement. Pierre was swept along in her enthusiasm and was ready to leave happier about the circumstances than he had been. They drove to the ferry departure jetty arriving by 7.30 am. The ferry was filled, fully booked, the early one a popular choice. The girl ran her finger down the bookings for the later departure. They could fit the car on the afternoon trip. Disappointed Pierre paid and booked on the 2 pm. boat. They had 6 hours to wait. Parking the Peugeot in the rapidly filling Port car park, they ambled into Toulon Centre, Marie Louise undismayed at the delay, Pierre anxious, his worry returning. He wanted to get away, here he felt too exposed.

Packer drove slowly into the rue de Magdelan. The mournful chimes of the Marie clock indicated 11 am. The road was not long, cluttered with cars and vans parked haphazardly. Packer pulled into a space and cut the engine. He had no idea where the apartment was.

Best to look for the girl, she would be known, probably lived here for some time. Packer walked into a dingy smoke filled bar. There were four women sipping early aperitifs morosely Packer asked the bar tender.

"Quite a few young women in the studios," he waved his hand vaguely at the shuttered houses across the roadway, "don't know their names, they come and go."

Packer drank his beer. He walked across and entered the dim hallway, eyes flicking over the name plates of the post boxes. The names meant nothing. He sighed, it meant another wait. As he stepped out a movement caught his eye. He glanced up. An old woman leaned on the sill of an open shuttered window, her black dress ruffled at the neck. Grey hair, unkempt her head swathed in a lace shawl. Her face was wrinkled and gaunt, her eyes bright and inquisitive.

'There's always one,' thought Packer, 'nothing else to do but watch and gossip.' He played a hunch.

"Bonj our Madame," Packer beamed at her. The head nodded.

"I'm looking for a young man. He's staying with his girlfriend, in a studio or apartment. Perhaps you know him?"

The old woman looked suspicious and said nothing. Packer went on. "He owes me some money, I did him a good turn and he's run off." Packer shrugged assessing her reaction.

He was right, the face scowled. "They're all the same

199

David-Penn

these days. No one pays, everyone takes your money. No one wants to pay." She went on bemoaning the fate of the old.

Packer nodded sympathetically. "I thought you may have seen him around."

"Over there," she nodded her head to the opposite buildings. "Only seen him once at the window, the girl's been there six months or more, works in a supermarket. Earns good money I expect. They all do these days and they spend it. Clothes, paint for their faces, trollops, all of them."

"Do you know which number?" Packer interrupted her ramblings.

The old head shook. "He's not there now, went out this morning with her carrying a case drove off in a car."

"What car, do you know the make?"

"Peugeot, I know a Peugeot, my grandson has one, same colour, brown. Thought it was him this morning, that's why I looked... Not from here though wasn't the 83 Region. Thirteen I think."

Packer smiled at her and blew a kiss, "Merci, Di es tres gentil."

The face twisted, Packer thought it was a smile. "Nice young man," she thought, "different to most of them." She continued peering at nothing, and everything.

Packer drove off annoyed he'd missed him again. At least he knew about the car. Thirteen, that was

200

Marseilles, it was the right lead. Carrying a case, could be going anywhere. Airport, Docks, probably back to Marseilles, then Spain, Tangiers, Christ knows... He'd just check the docks in Toulon, boats to Sardinia, Corsica, Italy perhaps, just perhaps. He drove steadily, eyes tuned in to all Peugeots checking registration numbers.

Yvonne was on edge she had arrived in plenty of time and was watching the crowded area for Brigitte and Brad Carter. At the same time she was conscious of the constant threat of Packer. There was no sign of Pierre.

Brad drew up and slid two euros into a parking meter, spotting Yvonne immediately. As he and Greg walked across she smiled with relief, recognising Brad. She walked to meet them.

'This is Greg," Yvonne smiled, Brigitte's description had been accurate, he was big.

"Let's have a coffee." Brad lead the way towards a small Bistro.

"Coffee's uncivilised at this time of day," muttered Greg, "I need a beer."

Yvonne was helpful, uninhibited, realizing she had someone on her side at last, now committed she answered all the questions and listened with wide eyes as the whole story was unfolded.

"I need to find Pierre," concluded Brad, "otherwise he will end up as Kleiber did."

"Well, his cars here. I was early so I looked around. It's there in the car park. I expect he's waiting for the ferry somewhere." They waited watching. Greg was quiet, frowning, disturbed.

They all saw the Audi drive into the car park without reaction. It meant nothing. Pierre and Marie Louise appeared from the crowd and walked towards the parking entry. Yvonne jumped up.

"There they are," she cried.

"Wait...!" Gregg pulled her back on her seat, "see what they do."

Yvonne was shaken by the hardness in Greg. They watched. Marie Louise and Pierre drove slowly out of the car park and drew in to the line of cars waiting to board the ferry. Tickets were checked and the line moved slowly into the gaping rear end of the boat, smoke whispering from the funnel. Yvonne was anxious, concerned, she had expected more than this lack of action. The Peugeot was beckoned on and disappeared into the bowels of the ferry. At that moment Yvonne gasped.

"He's here, the one who's after Pierre. Look over there the tall man in black." Brad and Greg looked up startled. Packer strolled out of the car park his eyes fixed on the disappearing car. Even from that distance they could see the vexation on his face.

"You're sure?" Brad was on his feet.

"Sit down," hissed Greg, "I've got an idea, do nothing.

Don't move, let Pierre go." Greg got up and moved quickly to the B.M.W. parked on the meter. He opened the door and collected his camera. The camera, battered and worn was always with him, the opportunity to take the unusual snap part of his training in the Newspaper world. He snapped the ferry, the line of cars, the crowds, and Packer. Acting like a tourist he snapped Packer again and again without making it obvious. Packer saw him but didn't notice. The heavy doors closed sullenly across the after end of the boat. Packer watched.

Greg hurried back to the table, "keep out of sight," he said quietly standing between Yvonne and Packer. "We must let Pierre go. Remember what I said Brad. Let him go. It's this bastard we want, not him. Believe me I know what I'm doing. Let's get out of here." Completely bewildered they followed Greg away from the dock area. The ferry whooped her siren and slid away from the jetty. Packer walked into the booking office.

"What is going on?" demanded Brad, "We chase all over the blasted Riveira trying to find this Pierre and when we finally run him to ground we slink away like a Vicar leaving a Brothel."

"Guile, dear old buddy guile, craft, cunning or sheer bloody luck, call it what you like. We now make the opposition work for us. Here..." Greg patted the camera hanging from his shoulder, "we have a photograph of the biggest killer since knicker elastic. I shall use all my irresistible charms to get this plastered across the front page of the Nice Matin. Public Enemy No 1, Police desperate to interview Sadistic killer, if seen do not approach. This man is dangerous... all that sort of crap."

Brad laughed, "You're not serious the paper would get sued till the editors shoes fell off. They'd never go along with it."

Greg grinned, "not quite as vehement as that perhaps but imagine if we blow his cover. Splash his ugly face in the paper. That would be enough. This guy works under cover. I bet hardly anyone knows him. If his face is revealed, the Mafia will blow him away. He'll be of no use, worse than that he'll be a liability. Dangerous to them, Joe Bloggs will suddenly vanish like passion at breakfast time."

"Speak for yourself," smiled Yvonne.

"Will your Editor go along Greg?" Brad began to see the logic behind the idea, "The paper must protect itself from libel?"

"Why not?" asked Greg, "all that is necessary to rebut a libel action is to prove that what is said is true. We know this guy is wanted by the police. I can't see Joe Bloggs retaining a lawyer to prove what a good boy he really is. There's no risk of action against the paper. All we want is his face staring at every reader. Don Vittorino will take off like the Space Shuttle."

"What about Pierre and Marie Louise?" Asked Yvonne, rather stunned by all the intrigue and heavy thinking. "If Joe blogs as you call him knows they have gone to Corsica he won't be far behind, he went into the booking office I watched him."

"Chances are that if I can get his face in the paper he won't dare to follow, at least not right away. Probably go into hiding for a week or so in case he is recognized. After a week people forget, he may try then. Greg looked at Brad, "I think you should let Pierre go Brad," he said seriously, apparently he didn't do anything too serious, the courts would certainly be more on his side than they will be on yours. Any guilt you want to wash away should start with Joe blogs."

Yvonne left them with a lighter heart, "I'll have a few days off," she grinned, "you never know business might improve."

Greg smiled, "That's what you said about passion at breakfast?"

Brad grabbed his arm and hustled him towards the car, "I'm not risking World War III with Brigitte."

Greg's charms were not as irresistible as he had imagined. Jules St. Germain his Editor flatly refused at first, calling the whole idea preposterous.

"I have no authority to even suggest that the police want to interview this man. They'll take me to pieces and feed me to their dogs. In any event the paper would be wide open for a libel action."

Greg argued for an hour, there was no chance of a libel action. The Mafia didn't call attention to themselves. Anyway the guy was guilty as hell the police knew it. Greg knew it, other people knew it. If he wasn't stopped he would kill again pretty damn soon. Finally they compromised St. Germain would print the photograph and when the police descended upon him he would insist that Greg: had lied, in which case Greg would be out of a job and St. Germain would be rid of another pain in the neck. The photographs proved to be clear and crisp. One, full face was enlarged and covered three columns of the front page. It made the midnight deadline.

The next morning Packer's face dominated the news-stands throughout the whole of the Var Region, the caption proclaiming that police were anxious to interview this man. It was hoped that he could assist with their enquiries regarding the death of one Hans Kleiber. Greg was delighted, St. Gerrnain waited for the building to fall on him.

Packer had watched the ferry slide away bitterly. Helpless, there was no way he could follow. He walked into the booking office and confirmed the destination of the ferry. He booked the first available vacancy to Ajaccio. There was no room until the next day at 2 pm. He shrugged, he had plenty of time. He booked into a hotel near the docks and relaxed over a large meal. Charging a full bottle of Cograc to his account he walked over to the reception desk. The night porter had just taken over. Packer slid 500 euros half way across the desk top.

"I'm in room 206, find me a woman who doesn't talk too much and there's another one of these for you... and for her," he added.

The porter grabbed the note which disappeared in a flash. "No problem Sir, Room 206 you said. Give her ten minutes."

"Make it nine," said Packer. He disappeared up the stairs. Packer was in the shower when the knock came. He wrapped a large bath towel around his waist and stepped out of the shower room, towelling his hair vigorously. "Entrez," he called.

A woman walked cautiously into the room and closed the door behind her. Packer stopped drying his hair and looked at her amazed. This was no dockside whore, she was beautiful. Tall and fresh, her light brown hair falling to her shoulders, her breasts full and thrusting beneath the silken blouse, her hips full and sensually curving into shapely nylon clad legs. She smiled noticing his surprise.

"You wanted a woman who doesn't talk too much," her voice was quiet, betraying her nervousness. Packer nodded, still affected by her there were no lines of hardness in her tanned face, her eyes were large and sad, her lips full and carefully rouged.

Packer found his voice, "you're no prostitute," he stated gruffly.

"I'm here to sleep with you, if you want me, for money, what does that make me?" she answered softly. "If I am not to talk, you are not to ask questions, enough to say that women have needs too, financial and physical."

Packer nodded conscious of a strange emotion in himself, his loins began to ache, needing her, but needing more the satisfaction of animal lust. He had used women, plenty of women, to satisfy the physical need. This was different. The spectre of isolation, loneliness, that was his whole existence, rose before him impossible this time to ignore, no longer thrust irritably from his mind, dominating his desires. Christ he wanted her. He held out a hand, pulling her gently to sit by him on the bed. He poured two glasses of brandy. Inside he was trembling, for Gods' sake.

Packer watched her undress, the skirt slipping to the floor with a faint rustle her breasts revealed nipples taut and hard as her blouse slid from her arms. She stood naked before him, she too trembling inwardly unsure, uncertain. Packer took her in his arms and covered her full mouth, sliding with her on to the bed pulling her soft yielding body close. She sensed his need, detected the controlled desperation responded urgently, her need as great, her thighs and inner self afire. He entered, their movements quickening into a frenzied passion, reaching a climax together which threatened to explode their minds. Packer clung to her his face burned in her breasts, their heartbeats hammering. Her fingers stroked his hair, still damp.

Later, the desire mutual they made love again. Packer coaxing her gently the desperation spent, only a deep desire remained. A desire to love her as the wind loves the trees. Caressing and responding to the murmurs and sighing gasps of her needs. They loved deep into the night oblivious of past and future until, as the early sun peeked inquisitively through the curtain chinks, they slept, enmeshed together warm in body and mind. She left as quietly as she had arrived, dressing carefully, not to wake Packer she was gone when he awoke. Her going left him desolate, he died a little more. He didn't even know her name. Exhausted he turned into the warm pillow her hair still fragrant where she'd laid. He slept.

Packer ate breakfast in his room, orange juice, croissants and coffee. Then it arrived, the porter delivered the newspapers as requested, The National La Monde and the Nice Latin. Packer opened the La Monde to the Petit announces, there was no message for him the headlines concerned further violence in Beirut. He pushed it aside and unfolded the Nice Latin, Packer froze, stupefied, his eyes widening with disbelief, his own features, clear and lifelike looked at him from the front page, as though the paper were a mirror. Frantic he read the caption printed below in heavy black type.

"Police anxious to interview this man It is believed he may be able to assist in enquiries concerning the death of Hans Kleiber, who was murdered recently in Manosque." Anxiously Packer searched for an accompanying news report, there was nothing, just the caption and the photograph, the damaging lethal photograph.

Packer's mind slid into top gear, how did the police

get this photograph, how did they know of him, connect him with Kleiber. No one saw him in Manosque he had been long gone when the body was found. He peered more closely at the photograph. There wasn't much, the features had been enlarged, the background cut away. In the gap between head and shoulder there was something, something out of focus. A building, a bar, it looked familiar, he had seen it before, the name was not there. Packer swore, he felt naked, trapped. Swiftly he showered and dressed. He must get out, the Porter would recognize him, the other staff. Perhaps the police were on their way already. He grabbed his small key grip and let himself out. Shunning the lift he moved quickly down the staircase. The reception desk was empty. He put the key and 500 euros on the register, enough to cover the cost of the room and a lot to spare. If the receptionist had connected him with the picture the tip might shut him up. Packer slid some heavily tinted sun glasses across his eyes. He felt the comfort of the slight security they offered. He walked quickly to the car park. There was no way he was going to Corsica. The prospect of mixing with crowds on the Ferry on the same day the photograph had appeared filled him with panic. From a thousand people one would surely recognise him. He must get away, away from the distribution of this bloody newspaper. As he crossed the road the memory of the day before flickered across his mind, watching the Peugeot rolling on to the ferry the crowds at the terminal, the big oaf snapping all that moved.

Camera, photographing, Packer stopped in his tracks. He gazed at the surrounding buildings his eyes pinpointing the Bar Restaurant overflowing with canvas chairs, the orange awning moving idly in the light wind. That was it. That was the bar in the photograph. Taken yesterday by the holidaymaker, only he wasn't a holidaymaker, Police? Hardly Police he would have been arrested there and then not photographed. Who was he? Packer couldn't recollect ever seeing him before? Two uniformed Gendarmes gossiped idly in front of him. He moved away and circled around them, desperate to reach the comparative security of the car. He drove slowly and carefully into the main exit, careful not to call attention to himself. Taking the exit to La Garde Packer made for the Nice-Aix en Provence Autoroute his mind frantic with questions, his stomach like ice. Never, never in all these years had his cover been blown. He had been careful, where had he gone wrong, who knew him.

Anyone who had been unlucky to pinpoint him in the past had been blown away. No one ever remained to identify him. The Mafia knew this, trusted him for this reason, safe from any dangerous connection themselves. Now half of bloody France knew him, Sacre peuter on all newspapers. His mind worked methodically, the fright of the moment passing into the cold cunning of self-preservation. Only two people knew who he was, Falaise the fat little git from the boatyard and the blonde tart. Both could identify him. Without their testimony the photograph was useless, intended to panic him. A Bar Tabac appeared ahead. He pulled in and parked, racks of newspapers stood outside the Bar entrance. His face stared back at him from the Nice Matin.

Christ the bloody paper was everywhere. He walked over and casually slid a copy of the War,' in front of the pack of the other Regional paper. The bar was quiet, two men noisily sipping coffee. They didn't even look at him. Packer lifted his hand, little finger and thumb extended to ear and mouth. The barman nodded jerking his thumb at the telephone at the end of the bar counter, he snapped a switch on the meter counter. Packer dialled the number of the Chantier Pegasus.' The phone rang out. There was no reply. He checked the number from a small letter covered note book. He dialled again, still nothing. Puzzled he looked at his watch, perhaps the little cow had gone out. He would wait telephones were scarce on this road far apart on the Autoroute. He nodded to the barman. "Rien."

The barman shrugged and blasted steam into a jug of milk. Packer sat in the car. He picked up the paper again scowling, searching again for any further information. The word Toulon caught his eyes. He read the short item.

"Accident on Toulon death strip on Thursday 14th Another accident occurred on the infamous three lane carriageway from canary to Six Fours, when a Renault five lost control and crashed off the highway. The driver M'sieu Jaccues Falaise was taken to Toulon Hospital

Generale where he was found to be suffering from shock and concussion and detained. This is the ninth accident to occur since the beginning of the month. Police are concerned and intend initiating strict speed controls."

Packer's eyes narrowed, in hospital, that's why there's no reply. He walked quickly back into the bar and thumbed through the Directory.

He dialled. "centre hospital..."

Packer became his most charming, "I would like to enquire about a friend who was injured in a street accident. His name is Falaise, Jacques Falaise. I believe the accident happened on the 14th."

"Lie quittez pas," The phone went quiet. Packer waited, "Putting you through to Doctor Neissler's Ward."

The Ward nurse answered. Packer repeated his request.

"M'sieu Falaise is recovering very well. He slept well and should be fit enough to leave hospital tomorrow, depending on the Doctors examination.

Can I give him a message?"

"You may speak with him if you wish."

"No thank you," replied Packer, "as long as he is ok I'll see him when he comes out."

Packer hung up, the Audi turned back towards

Toulon self-preservation the only thought in his mind. His future depended on eradicating identification. Without anonymity he was unemployable, he laughed, unemployable. He was a dead man walking... the Mafia would not forgive. He was a menace to the organisation, a weak link, weak links were intolerable in the chain... he would be disposed of, what did they call it, Expedient demise.

Packer had blasted away many weak links himself. His only hope was to convince Don Vittorino that all risks were neutralised. Falaise and the girl must go, quickly and completely. Pierre could wait, there would be time for him. The only two who could identify him took first priority.

Chapter 22

Inspector Dubois was livid. Pacing up and down in his office his normally placed features diffused with heat. He glared at the Nice Matin. There had been no instructions given to the paper to publish any photograph. The Police didn't even know of the photograph. Where the hell had it come from? Merde, merde.' He picked up the phone and snapped at the switchboard.

"Get me the editor of the Nice Matin," he fumed.

Jules St. Germain had been expecting a call ever since he arrived at work. Seeing the daily edition he had regretted the impulse which had allowed him to be persuaded by Greg. He cursed. The phone jangled.

"Nice police for you Jules." Jules gritted his teeth.

Dubois didn't beat about the bush. "Who gave you the authority to publish the photograph and state that the police were anxious to interview this man?"

Jules sounded astonished. "I was fully under the impression that your Department had done so Inspector, isn't it true?"

"You know bloody well it isn't true, where did you get this picture."

"I was informed that the man can help police. You

know we do all we can to assist the Law. One of our reporters spotted him. We have some very keen reporters."

Dubois took a deep breath. "Perhaps you don't realize that our investigation has been seriously jeopardized by premature exposure. I could have you thrown into the Bastille for this. For so long your grand-children would die of old age before you came out."

Jules adopted a more offensive attitude. "You admit that the man is wanted, you need to interview him, that he is a possible criminal?"

Dubois hesitated, he didn't want to give any more away than he had to, "Perhaps," he replied cautiously, "but only when I say so, not when you lunatic journalists decide for me."

Jules grinned, he sensed the Achilles heel. "If we have been a bit premature I apologise. Only trying to help freedom of the Press and all that," he added maliciously, "I'll publish the photo again and add an apology, police are not yet ready to interview this man.'

Dubois nearly burst a blood vessel. "Don't you bloody dare! You do nothing without official permission, which will be very difficult to obtain," he added darkly. "You haven't heard the end of this!" He slammed the phone back on the cradle.

Yvonne marched gaily into the hospital carrying a plastic bag. She had bought a tin of cigars and a box of fancy patisseries. 'Make him fatter than ever,' she thought, 'but it would help her get a few days off.' She rode in the elevator joining the evening visitors. Jacques was pleased to see her although he didn't show it. No one had been near him since Pierre and he was fed up with the hospital. His temperature had been too high for him to be discharged as yet, he hoped for the next day...

He listened avidly as Yvonne covered the happenings with Brad and Greg, frowning anxiously as he heard about Packer and the fact that Pierre had been seen leaving for Corsica.

"Why take that little floozy with him. I told him to stay on his own. Safer that way..."

He groped through the box of cakes and chose a creamy concoction. Packer also entered the hospital, gauging his entrance to coincide with visiting hours. Unnoticed in the regular movement of people, he walked purposefully along corridors, carrying a bunch of flowers, his eyes searching. Packer found what he was seeking, a door, clearly marked. 'Laverie' He tried the door, it opened. There was no one to see him slip in. The room contained bins overflowing with used bed linen, pillow cases and pyjamas. He saw what he was looking for, white medical coats, thrown haphazard in a corner bin. He sorted through them selecting one to fit him. The flowers he threw in the corner and slipped into the coat. The Magnum slid from the shoulder holster, Packer screwed a silencer into the barrel. He pushed the gun into his waist band and buttoned the coat. There would be no time for finesse this must be fast and final, then for the girl. He opened the door cautiously, the corridor was empty. He walked firmly towards the staircase, past a trolley laden with syringes and bottles. A clip board holding charts rested on the top, Packer picked it up as he passed now slowing. Doctor Neissler's Ward was on the third floor, one floor above. He mounted the stairs avoiding the visitors who were beginning to leave.

Packer swung back the heavy plastic doors and walked into the ward corridor. He didn't know the room. There were not too many patient rooms. With a confident air he opened the first and glanced in, wrong room, he closed the door. The next two were open, occupied he came to 319. No one challenged him, no nurses were around anxious to get rid of the visitors the sight of another Doctor was not unusual. He wasn't even noticed.

Packer opened 319. Jacques Falaise was sat propped up in the bed, Yvonne standing preparing to leave. A young nurse was tidying the bed in the corner. There was no one else in the room. The whole scene imprinted itself on Packer's mind as he slid into the room closing the door behind him. The Girl was there, a bonus, Falaise's jaw dropping as he recognised Packer, Yvonne opening her mouth to scream, the nurse bending across the bed, her face turned without expression. Packer fired, the Magnum leaping into his hand coughing three times.

The first bullet slammed into Falaise thrusting him

back into the pillows, the box of cakes erupting into the air, the next knocked Yvonne backwards into the chair, collapsed, soundless shocked disbelief distorting her face. The third bullet transformed the nurse's face into a blood smeared mask she was dead before she slid to the floor. It was 10 seconds since Packer entered the room. Thrusting the still smoking gun into his trouser band he opened the door and walked calmly out, calling a fatuous remark over his shoulder. He closed the door. If anyone had heard the muffled shots they gave no sign. No attention was paid to Packer as he left the ward. Two minutes later the Audi pulled away and vanished into the evening traffic.

Packer was elated, to get the girl as well, one hit and the two were gone. He spared no thought for the nurse, she was just unlucky. Now he was clear, risk of discovery eliminated, no longer a weak link in the chain, one more thing to do. Don Vittorino must know. Must be convinced the threat to the organisation no longer existed. Packer looked for a telephone. He dialled the number form a roadside phone box. Vittorino answered.

"We must talk," Packer said quietly, "the goods have been despatched. There is no record of the despatcher."

"I agree" Vittorino's voice was cold, ominous. "Here, tonight." he hung up. Packer frowned, he had not envisaged going to Vittorino, expecting to meet elsewhere. He drove towards Cannes, less sure, the worm of suspicion crawling in his gut.

Vittorino glanced at Packer then his watch, he flicked

a switch and a large television screen glowed and came to life. He selected FR.3 there were five minutes to wait for Soir 3, the late night news. Packer was nonchalant, confident that he had tied up enough ends to avoid any association with the trail of violence. There was no risk to the organisation. Vittorino listened, holding his hand up to stop Packer speaking when the news came on. The T.V. Station carried the story.

"At the hospital the blood bath had been discovered by the Senior Infirmiere checking that all visitors had left, or were leaving. The mutilated face of the dead nurse coupled with two bodies bleeding profusely had thrown her into terrified hysterics. Within moments the ward was a mass of people. Yvonne and Falaise were rushed to the theatre for emergency surgery. The Police arrived within minutes and the whole hospital was sealed off. Everyone leaving was checked, bags examined and searched. Frightened visitors were ushered out of the wards, many unaware of what was going on. The staff confined to one ward while rooms were searched thoroughly. The flowers were found but yielded no clue. The television crews, there within a short time were restricted to the outer areas, frantic to interview and to film everything, the whole hospital a blaze of light, the flashing blue police car lamps added to the frenzied scenes. An unkempt news reporter, appeared on the screen clutching a microphone his eyes reflected the flashing lights, gave a garbled account of the horror in room 319. The nurse was dead, terrible injuries to her head. A patient, as yet unnamed and a young woman visitor were in a very serious condition, the extent of their injuries yet to be determined. The attack appears to be that of a maniac, no reason or motive for the possible triple murder. Checks at the hospital so far had yielded no clue. The investigations were continuing.

Don Vittorino switched off the set. His eyes were cold and expressionless. "So they are not dead?" he murmured quietly, "just the nurse who was of no importance."

Packer was disturbed. He knew he was good, never missed. The cold professional in him excelled at times of stress. He had not missed, had seen the bullets strike, a 357 left little leeway. He shrugged with a confidence he didn't feel.

"They will die, perhaps are dead by now, there is no need to worry."

Don Vittorino sighed, he steepled his fingers, looking at Packer unblinkingly. "You realize the situation you have created. Your photograph is spread across the Riviera, within a short time you will be directly associated with all the deaths, including these," he gestured towards the set. "The police are not fools, they will unravel everything, complete the jigsaw puzzle, slot in the last piece. That last piece could be me." He lifted his hand and his eyes blazed stopping an indignant retort from Packer. "You must not continue with this assignment, the man in Corsica must be left alone. There can be no further assignments for you within my organisation, you must disappear tonight, leave France, leave Europe, at least for a year. I cannot allow any possibility of a weak link (the expression sent a shiver through Packer) risking all I have built up. You have sufficient funds your services have been invaluable in the past. Now we must part, our lives must diverge, there will, no doubt be a place for you elsewhere. There is no longer a place for you here."

Don Vittorino rose the determination obvious in his attitude. There was no point in arguing. At least there was to be no expedient demise yet, Packer's senses tensed. It would not do to be too confident of that. Vittorino's manner changed. The hard aloof attitude dropped from him, he offered another drink. Packer refused still uncomfortable. He left escorted to the door, expecting the man with the shot gun to accompany him. There was no one in sight.

Vittorino shook his hand, "sorry about the car, self-preservation," he smiled.

The huge door closed quietly Packer walked down the steps. The light from the house behind him emphasising the darkness ahead. He stopped for a moment to adjust his vision, listening, senses taught, he still wasn't sure, there was something. Avoiding the gravel road he stepped quietly on to the grass verge, he moved silently and fast, eyes flicking at every shadow, watching for movement ears straining for the smallest sound. There was none, darkness and silence, a deep screaming silence. He glided towards the Gates. Packer felt, rather than heard the sound. He stopped, ears and eyes straining. It came again, a rustling, urgent, movement. Movements spread across the darkness to his right. His blood chilled there it was again, closer, he heard a muffling gurgle, a slight throaty growl. The rushing turned to weighty padding. "Dogs, dogs for Christ sake...!" Packer ran, swift footed, swerving across the roadway to his left, his hand groping for his gun. He cursed, remembering they had taken it. The sounds were nearer identifiable now, the snarling anticipation of killer dogs the shrubbery crackled aid parted at their eager progress. How many...the sounds seemed to cover a wide arc.

Packer raced into the trees desperate to find cover. He leapt at an overhanging branch grabbing desperately as the bough sagged. He swung his legs violently upwards. The first dog to reach him leapt like a black torpedo from the darkness. The faint light glistening on the bared fangs, flecked tongue extended from the wide jaws. The teeth sunk deep into Packer's thigh ripping flesh, closing on the bone the weight and momentum dragging his hands from the branch tumbling him into a screaming terrified heap on the ground. The other dogs converged at the same time, the fear ridden shrieks ending abruptly as Packer's throat was torn apart. The dogs savaged the body long after death, making no sound apart from a glutinous snuffling of satisfaction. After minutes they padded softly away into the darkness leaving the barely recognizable body deep in the bushes. The weak link had snapped.

Chapter 23

The Audi was driven some distance away, the man threw a pair of driving gloves on the seat and wiped the steering wheel clean. The gloves would explain the complete absence of finger prints. He slammed the door, leaving the keys and cleaned the door handle. The side door slammed behind him, the red sign caught the street lamps glow.

He reported to Don Vittorino. "An intruder sir, probably a burglar, must have climbed the wall, the dogs got him. No idea who he is but he's very dead."

Don Vittorino nodded his lips firm. He dialled the police. Inspector Dubois arrested Greg and Brad. Two plain clothes officers called at the apartment very early the next morning, careful to explain that Inspector Dubois wished to speak with them. They could attend willingly or be taken into custody. "Inspector Dubois asked me to say," I don't give a damn which they choose," one police officer grinned maliciously.

Two very chastened men sat waiting in the Inspector's office some time later, visions of a very uncomfortable future ahead of them passing through their minds and conversation.

"He's got no right to arrest us. We've not continued any crime, there's nothing he can do. I shall raise one big goddamned stink about this," muttered Greg.

Brad looked at him. "I agree with you but I'm not making any plans for the next ten years."

The Inspector walked in. They both shut up and looked at him sheepishly. Dubois said nothing, fixing the pair with a stony gaze. He sat down and sorted papers on his desk. The silence was oppressive. After a few minutes Dubois looked up, his face serious, his manner very professional.

"Well," he said sardonically. "How are you amateur extensions of justice feeling? So far you are responsible for six murders, two people living in fear of their lives, the total disintegration of months of dedicated police work and the initiation of a full scale enquiry in to the security systems operative within the country's hospitals. The serious debilitation of the nervous system of one very unhappy, and very angry police Inspector, that's for starters and should qualify you both for a rat infested hole in the depths of the Bastille until the next French Revolution."

Brad started to protest. "Silence," roared Dubois. With an effort he controlled himself. Brad sat dumbstruck.

"Last night I viewed the body of a young innocent girl, a nurse at Toulon hospital. Two more people lay in the shadow of death in intensive care! Late last night very late last night I was presented with the macerated remains of your photographic model, ripped to shreds by Vittorinos guard dogs. I am terrified of what tomorrow may bring unless I either lock you both away from sight for ever or blow my own brains out."

Seeing the shocked faces, Dubois explained what had taken place, quietly and venomously.

"I am not joking gentlemen," he went on quietly, "your activities however well-intended have been seriously misplaced. Left to the forces of law and order, the original culprits would have been brought to book. Other lives would have been saved. Innocent people would not have been involved and your own consciences would have been less heavy on your minds than I am sure they are. It is because I am sure of this last fact that I shall take no action. I could throw the book at both of you and make it stick but I shall not. I leave your punishment to self-recrimination. Remember the oldest and wisest advice ever given to mankind, 'Vengeance is mine saith the Lord.' If I ever see either of you, or hear of you, or God forbid become entangled with you again, I shall adopt the mantel of the Lord myself and exact the most terrible Vengeance, enough to make even thin sit up."

By a miracle of modern surgery both Yvonne and Jacques Falaise lived. Yvonne had been luckier than Jacques, the bullet had smashed her ribs and been diverted away from her chest cavity by the slight turn she had made, her reactions twisting her at the moment of the bullet slamming into Jacques. With Jacques the tearing metal had ripped his stomach apart and exited within millimetres of his spine. Massive and continual repair brought about an almost complete recovery. They both spent weeks in the hospital subjected to interviews by the press and the news media much to Yvonne's ultimate delight and Jacques blasphemous criticism. Brigitte had listened with glee to the account of the interview with Inpector Dubois, nodding her head in aggravating agreement as each criticism unfolded.

"You're as bloody bad as he is," growled Greg, Brad was silent, deeply affected.

"Well" said Brigitte, "perhaps you will both mind your own business now, stick to those things you're both good at." She glanced at the generous glasses of whisky they were both sipping miserably, like boozing and writing up fashion shows in your papers. I'm going out."

Greg looked up. "Where are you off to?"

"Toulon hospital, I'm going to take Yvonne a huge bunch of flowers and big kiss to say you're both sorry." Brigitte shrugged into her leather coat.

"Take care then," grunted Greg, "don't want you getting lost."

Brigitte grinned, "You should be so lucky, remember that other very wise saying, "never resist the inevitable, it could contain the fruits of great enjoyment."

"I don't remember Confucius saying that," said Greg startled.

"He didn't," chuckled Brigitte, "I did." She swung through the door.

Brad chuckled, the chuckle turned into a suppressed laugh which built into a deep spasm of wholesome laughter. Greg looked at him and smiled, the infectious sound impossible to resist, he too laughed. Within moments they were both holding themselves and roaring with hilarity, tears pouring from their eyes. With Brad they were not all tears of laughter.

DAVID PENN

A Grave Matter
— in —
Hampton Pogmore

DAVID PENN

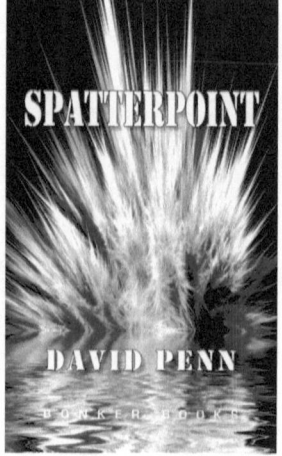

SPATTERPOINT

DAVID PENN

BUNKER BOOKS

David Penn

www.Bonkerbooks.com